AMISH WIDOW'S SECRET

EXPECTANT AMISH WIDOWS BOOK 9

SAMANTHA PRICE

CHAPTER 1

But seek ye first the kingdom of God, and his righteousness;
and all these things shall be added unto you.
Matthew 6:33

CASSANDRA YODER STOOD ROOTED to the spot and stared at the home where she'd grown up. It was a white house with a red roof, pretty much the same as all the other farmhouses in the area. Upstairs were five bedrooms that had housed her parents, five older sisters, herself and her younger sister. Now the only child left at home was Gretchen, the youngest daughter. Cassandra had always been different, always felt different, from the rest of the family. Her mother used to say to her all the time, *'I don't know who you take after,'* and, *'You're nothing like the rest of the familye.'*

A ruby-throated hummingbird with its long curved

beak flitted from flower to flower, drawing Cassandra's attention away from her melancholy thoughts.

The main difference between her family home and every other Amish home in the area was the garden that her mother lovingly tended every day. It was spring and the blooms were out in full flower.

Cassandra looked down at the bag at her feet, which the taxi driver must have placed there before he drove away. She was in a daze. She'd never wanted to come back here—back to the Amish, but now she had nowhere else to go. There was no one else to turn to.

She'd left on *rumspringa* with her childhood friend, Jake, who had become, over their teenage years, her boyfriend. They'd stayed together until recently. Jake had returned to the community leaving Cassandra to pay the entire rent on their small apartment. He'd wanted to get married and for the two of them to return to the community together. That wasn't the only difference of opinion they'd had.

Now that she was standing in front of the house, she wondered how she would feel facing her parents and the rest of the community, considering that she hadn't gone to Jake's funeral.

The same week that Jake had gone back to the Amish he'd been killed in an armed hold-up at a gas station. Jake had been there to buy a bottle of soda and a stray bullet had killed him instantly. She still hadn't forgiven him for leaving her and their unborn child and besides that she couldn't face the scrutiny of Bishop Joel, her parents, or the Amish community.

Now she knew she would have to face their judgment;

she couldn't see any other way around it. Cassandra knew her parents would be deeply ashamed of her once they found out she was expecting a child out of wedlock. Jake and she had been living as man and wife from the time they had left the community. While they had lived in the community, they had gotten along fine, but the financial pressures and the *Englisch* world had made their differences come to light all too vividly. They both realized they had nothing in common and were unsuited to be a couple.

Jake could never understand why Cassandra didn't want to return to the community. After a final row, Jake had walked out on her and their baby. He'd talked about leaving her for months, maybe hoping that would change her mind, before he left for good. Even the news that he was going to be a father didn't make him stay with her. Jake deserted her, leaving her alone—an unmarried mother—without the marriage vows but as good as a widow.

Thankfully, Jake hadn't told anybody about her pregnancy. She knew that for a fact because no one in the community had reached out to her.

Her tummy flip-flopped just thinking about how her parents would react to her news. She knew she couldn't keep the baby and neither did she want to, but would her parents try to make her keep the child? They would be so embarrassed by her condition and worried about their reputation; that's one thing Cassandra knew for sure and for certain.

But she'd had to come home. Her waitressing job didn't pay much and then her hours had been cut right back. With Jake gone, without his income, all the bills had added up and some of them were now left unpaid.

She hadn't seen her family since she left nearly two years ago. Now she realized that she should've kept in touch with them. It was awkward just landing on the doorstep like this and expecting them to open their arms and welcome her home after she'd turned her back on them. Now she knew what it felt like to have someone turn their back; Jake had done so to her and their unborn child.

When Cassandra had been a young girl, she knew she would marry Jake and Jake felt the same back then, but it wasn't to be. She was now alone and facing the world with the biggest problem she could ever imagine a woman having to face.

If she could turn back the clock, she wouldn't have taken that apartment with Jake. She would've taken one with another girl. It had been a silly move to live together as man and wife, but she'd thought she knew him. It was most likely the guilt that they'd both felt from living together that finally drove them apart. Nevertheless, the Jake she thought she knew would've stood by her no matter what. She was bitterly disappointed in Jake and that was the reason she hadn't gone to his funeral.

CHAPTER 2

While the earth remaineth, seedtime and harvest,
and cold and heat, and summer and winter,
and day and night shall not cease.
Genesis 8:22

THE FRONT DOOR OPENED, and a young woman stood in the doorway and then took a step out onto the porch. It was Gretchen—she'd grown taller and thinner. Gone was the chubby-cheeked girl she'd argued with nearly every day of her life.

Gretchen wore a purple dress with starched white apron and starched white prayer *kapp*. She was a perfect picture, just as always. Cassandra was now all too aware that she was wearing jeans that she was busting out of, a tee shirt and high-heeled boots. If she were really going to do this and return home, she'd have to resume wearing dresses and *kapps*.

If there was one thing she'd been pleased to see the end of when she left the community, it was wearing the dratted *kapp* day in and day out. More than the *kapp,* she hated what it represented. It symbolized man having the rule over women and that is something she refused to believe. She was going to be her own boss and no one would 'lord it' over her and tell her what to do; not her parents, not her older sisters, and not Jake."

There was no hint of a smile on Gretchen's face when she stepped forward and asked, "What are you doing back home?"

The question was worthy of an answer. Gretchen clearly hadn't changed. "Where are *Mamm* and *Dat?"*

"Dat's working and *Mamm's* here somewhere."

Cassandra looked down at the bag by her feet, took a deep breath, and then took hold of the handle and stepped forward to walk inside.

Gretchen moved to block her way. "Are you moving back?"

"What's it to you?"

"I live here and I didn't leave. Did you write and ask *Mamm* and *Dat* if you could come back?"

"Get out of my way, Gretchen."

"Or what?"

"Or I'll drop this bag on your toe and I can tell you right now it's pretty heavy." Cassandra stared at Gretchen until she moved out of the way. "Finally!" Cassandra said as she stepped through the doorway past Gretchen. She walked in the door and dropped her bag on the floor. *"Mamm!"* she hollered.

"Just as selfish as always, leaving your bag right there instead of taking it up to your room."

Cassandra swung around to face her sister. "Why don't you take it up to my room for me?"

"I don't have to take orders from you."

"Well stop complaining, then."

"Cassie, is that you?"

Cassandra heard her mother's voice calling from the top of the stairs. "Yeah, *Mamm,* it's me."

She flew down the stairs and when she got to the bottom, she ran to her daughter. She wrapped her arms around her. "I knew you'd come back to us."

"She's probably only here because she's got no other place to go. That's my guess," Gretchen said.

"Stop it, Gretchen. You should be pleased to see your sister back home. Now, run and tell your *vadder* that our Cassie has come home to us."

Cassandra's mother being shorter than all her daughters looked up into Cassandra's face. "You are staying, aren't you?"

"*Jah* I'm staying for awhile, but I don't know how long." Cassandra took a look at her younger sister. "*Mamm* told you to tell *Dat* I'm here. That's what *Mamm* said, now go."

"Okay, I'm going." Gretchen headed off into the fields to get her father.

"Cassandra, I'm so happy to see you. I knew you'd come back to us one day."

"I need to talk to you and *Dat* about something important. I've got myself into a situation and I need to figure out how to get out of it."

"Do you owe people money?"

"*Jah,* but that's not the main problem. I owe a couple of weeks rent and a few things like that, but that doesn't matter."

Her mother gasped. "It does matter. You can't owe people money. That's dreadful."

"Well, if you're so upset about it, you can pay the debts off. It's only a few hundred dollars."

Her mother touched her stomach. "A few hundred dollars? That's a lot of money. Why would you think your *vadder* and I would pay it for you?"

"Well I don't care about it; if you do, you can pay it."

Her mother frowned at her and Cassandra knew what her mother was thinking—she'd heard it all before. *I can't believe I ever had a daughter like you. I don't know where you come from. Sometimes I wonder if you're really mine with your sharp tongue and your dark hair.* Everyone else in the family had blonde hair or strawberry blonde; Cassandra was the only dark haired one in the whole family.

"No one touched my room, did they? I bet Gretchen took it over."

"We haven't done anything to your room. It's just the same as you left it except it's cleaner, of course, and the bed is made."

"Why do you have to throw things like that in my face? I suppose I left the bed unmade? I can't believe you've been holding a grudge like that for so long."

"Cassandra, you never made your bed. I'm simply pointing that out to you, and you always left your room in a filthy state. None of your sisters did that, ever."

"I'm sorry, *Mamm,* I'm just tired and cranky. I never want to argue."

Her mother smiled at her. "Come into the kitchen and I'll fix you a glass of meadow tea."

The reason Cassandra didn't want to argue was that she knew in a few minutes she'd be telling both of her parents something that would upset them greatly. There was no point in arguing about not making her bed years ago.

Cassandra's father came through the door just as she had sat down at the kitchen table.

"There's my girl," he said as he hurried toward her.

She stood up and he hugged her for a moment before she pushed him away. *"Dat,* you're all sweaty and smelly. Phew!"

"He's been working, that's why," her mother said.

"It's good to see you, *Dat."*

Her father said, "You never visit us. Does this mean you're home for good now?"

"That depends on the both of you. I need to have a talk with you."

"Jah, it will be interesting to hear what you have to say," Gretchen said.

She looked up to see her sister with her arms folded, leaning against the kitchen wall.

"I'm not talking with you. I said I want to talk with *Mamm* and *Dat*. I don't want you to be here at all."

"Now girls, stop arguing at once," her mother said.

"Gretchen, you go up to your room for half an hour," her father ordered.

"Why am I getting punished? I haven't done anything. I've always been here and I've never left. *She's* been gone for two years doing exactly as she pleases, and you treat her real nice when she comes back? It's not fair!"

Her mother glared at her. "Life's not meant to be fair. It's best you learn that early!"

"Go to your room, Gretchen," her father repeated in a calm voice.

Mrs. Yoder added, "You're not being punished; we just want to speak with your *schweschder* in private."

"I'm part of the family. I don't see why I can't listen in."

"Just go," Mr. Yoder said.

Gretchen pouted and then walked out of the room.

CHAPTER 3

Ask, and it shall be given you;
seek, and ye shall find;
knock, and it shall be opened unto you:
Matthew 7:7

CASSANDRA'S MOTHER placed three glasses of meadow tea on the table.

"Denke." Cassandra took a sip of the sweet mint-infused meadow tea. When she placed the glass down on the table, she realized there was no going back. She looked from one parent to the other. "I've got something to tell you and neither of you is going to like it." She took a deep breath. "The thing is, I'm having a *boppli."*

"Nee!" Her mother put her hand over her heart with a pained expression on her face as though she were having a heart attack.

"And in case you're wondering, it's Jake's. Not that he

cared about it, he just walked out and left me to pay all the bills and the rent on our apartment."

"He knew about this?" her father asked.

"*Jah,* he knew about it and he deserted me without a care. He said he wanted to come back to the community and he owed me nothing if I didn't return with him." She shook her head. She had to make her parents see how horrible it had been for her, after living with Jake for so long.

Both parents sat there stunned, so Cassandra thought she should fill the silence with words of explanation. "We got along before we left the community. He wasn't the person I thought he was. He changed."

"He can't answer for himself now, so it's best you don't speak about him in that way," her father said. "Now, you have to figure out what you're going to do."

"What *I'm* going to do? I'm only telling you because I want you both to tell me what you think I should do. I can't keep it. I don't want it." Cassandra scowled at the thought of looking after a child.

"Tell me this, did you come back because you wanted to return to the community or because you need our help?" he asked.

"I don't know. Does it really matter?"

"It matters a great deal. We'll help you, but it's your relationship with *Gott* I'm more concerned about rather than earthly matters."

"This time, *Dat,* I need your help. It's important because whether you like it or not there's going to be a *boppli.* You have to help me figure out what to do, or I'll just dump it somewhere. I thought you and *Mamm* would at least help me find it a decent home."

Her mother lifted herself from her chair. "Stop calling the *boppli* an 'it.' Your *boppli* is a small person already." Once she'd made her point, her mother sat back down. Tears fell down her face and she wiped them away with the back of her hand.

Cassandra's father moved to sit next to his wife and he placed his arm around her. "It's okay, Thelma, we'll get through this."

Cassandra jumped up. "*You'll* get through this? You're acting like this is your problem, but it's *my* problem. It's happening to *me!* Or are you worried about what people will say? Is that it? Is that all you care about?"

"Sit down, Cassandra," her father ordered. "I've got no patience for your antics. We'll help you figure out what to do, but as your parents, we're supposed to be leading and guiding you in the right way to live. We've failed with you."

"I can figure that out for myself. I'm not a child anymore. I'll have the baby and then figure out what I wanna do with my life. I might stay in the community and I might not. Who knows?" Cassandra knew very well that she didn't want to stay in the community, but now was not the time or place to tell her parents that. She needed their help, and having them think she was going to stay on in the community was the best way she knew to get it.

"Have you thought about adoption?" Thelma asked, seeming to have gotten rid of all her tears.

"I think that's probably best. I could abort, but then I might feel bad about it later."

"Nee, you mustn't do that," Thelma said.

"How far along are you?" her father asked.

"About three months."

Her father and mother exchange glances; she knew they were thinking that she might soon start to show.

"I think the best solution is to send you to Aunt Maud's. You can have the baby there and she'll help you find a suitable family for adoption."

"You're sending me away? That's not what I came here for."

"If you stay here, everyone will know. They'll all find out."

"So what?" Cassandra asked, knowing the answer already.

"Your *vadder* and I have been in this community since we were small children, and we're well thought of in the community…"

"Oh. I see. I thought that was it. You're worried about what everyone will think. You're not so much worried about me, and what will happen to me. You're worried about your own reputations within the community."

Her mother's gaze lowered to the kitchen table.

"If you'd given any thought to your own reputation you wouldn't have gotten yourself into this mess. You talked Jake into going away with you and then the next thing we hear is that you're living together. Then you return and we are supposed to fix all the problems that you have caused?"

"So my baby is a problem?"

"Your *vadder* didn't mean that. Each child is a blessing from *Gott."*

"Is my child a blessing?"

"Your child might be a blessing for a childless *familye,*" her mother said. "So, *jah.*"

"I suppose it's my fault that Jake was shot?"

"We're not saying that, but it's possible that he wouldn't have been at that gas station on the way to a job interview," her mother said.

It appeared that her father disagreed. "It was his time to go."

Cassandra looked at her father. At least he was on her side about something.

"Do I even know Aunt Maud?" Cassandra asked.

"Maud came here when you were just a little girl," her father said.

"And she's one of your older sisters isn't she, *Dat?*"

"*Jah,* she is. All her *kinner* are grown up and moved away and she's happy to have visitors."

"How do you know she'll help me?"

"She will."

"Your *mudder* will write to her tonight and I'll post the letter tomorrow. We'll tell her your circumstances and ask her to find a *gut familye* for the *boppli.*"

Cassandra was silent. It seemed a good idea now that she had a little moment to think it through. She could go and have the baby away from this community and no one would be any the wiser and it didn't mean she had to come back and stay in the community. She could leave if she wanted to.

"So you're not going to tell anybody in the community here about me being pregnant? We're keeping it hush-hush—on the 'down low'?"

Her mother nodded, and added, “This is no joke.”

Cassandra nodded. “I know. More than anyone, I know that.”

“It's best to keep these things just between *familye.* I don’t want anyone else to know only us three and Maud and Uncle Max," Mr. Yoder said.

"I thought you'd want the bishop to know, *Dat.”*

"Nee, this is something I wouldn’t want anybody to find out.”

Her father looked down at the palms of his hands and Cassandra knew he was very disappointed in her. The bishop and he were good friends and her father strived to be a Godly man. Heavy lines had appeared in her mother’s forehead. Her mother was disappointed in her more than anything else. Cassandra shrugged off her parents’ attitudes. What did they expect would happen when she was living with Jake in a one-bedroom apartment?

Her father stood up. "It's good to see you home, Cassandra, no matter what the circumstances. Sometimes *Gott* tries us to see what we are made of."

Cassandra’s father always made everything about God. She was tempted to say she didn't like a God, who would make bad things happen to people to teach them a lesson. She kept quiet because she needed her parents to be on her side just this one time.

As her father was going out the back door, he said, "I've got some things to do, but we’ll talk more later."

"Okay, *denke, Dat.”*

He called over his shoulder, “Get changed into some normal clothes."

She looked down at her jeans and tee-shirt.

"We've got some of your clothes upstairs. I think you'd better change into them."

"I don't. I came back to visit—that doesn't mean I'm going back to the meetings and being a part of everything again."

"Just get out of those clothes. And please stop arguing with everything I say, Cassandra. It's quite exhausting."

Cassandra sighed and tied her dark hair into a knot at the nape of her neck.

"I'll fix you something to eat while you go upstairs and get changed."

Cassandra stood up, leaned over and kissed her mother on the cheek. *"Denke, Mamm.* I'm sorry I'm so hard to get along with sometimes. I knew I could count on you. I knew you'd know what to do."

Her mother smiled. "Isn't that what *mudders* are supposed to do?"

"I guess so," Cassandra said as she walked out of the room.

CHAPTER 4

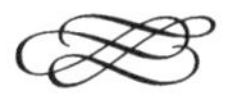

I am not ashamed: for I know whom I have believed,
and am persuaded that he is able to keep that
which I have committed unto him against that day.
2 Timothy 1:12

CASSANDRA WALKED into her bedroom and saw that it was the same as she'd left it with one exception, and that was that the bed was now made. Her clothes were hanging on the same pegs by the door. There was one purple dress one yellow dress and a dark green dress. She lifted the yellow dress off the peg, and slumped onto the bed with the dress in her hands.

"Now I know why you're home."

She looked up to see her younger sister.

"You were listening in after *Dat* told you it was a private conversation? You'll probably go to Hell for that."

"I'm going to hell? If I am, what about you?" Gretchen

asked.

Cassandra glared at her sister.

Gretchen added, "I'm not a little girl anymore and you can't scare me about hell. It's not my fault that I can hear everything from my bedroom and you've all got loud voices."

She had a point. Gretchen sat down on the bed with Cassandra. "Are you really having a *boppli?*"

"*Jah,* I am, but *Mamm* and *Dat* don't want anybody to know. They're sending me away to Aunt Maud's."

"Who's Aunt Maud?"

"*Dat's* older *schweschder.* I vaguely remember her. I think she was nice, but when I was younger, I thought everybody was nice."

"Are you gonna give the *boppli* away?

Cassandra nodded. "I guess so."

"And it's Jake's?"

"If you've been listening in you'd know the answer to that. Why even ask me?"

"I'm trying to be nice, Cassandra. I don't know what else to say."

"You're only trying to be nice because you feel sorry for me. You don't need to feel sorry for me."

"How can you give your *boppli* away?"

"It's the only kind thing to do. I wouldn't be a *gut mudder,* and the *vadder* is dead. So, it's the logical thing to do."

"You could give the *boppli* to me."

Cassandra laughed. "Why would I do that? You wouldn't be able to raise it any better than I could. And besides that, you're only twelve."

"I'm not twelve, and you know it. I'll be eighteen at the end of the year. I could marry someone and keep the *boppli*."

"I didn't know you were so keen on babies."

"Neither did I until I heard you were going to give yours away. The *boppli* will be my niece or nephew."

"Don't be so dramatic! You're making this about you, and it's not about you, it's about me. You're so self-absorbed. You've always been jealous of me."

Gretchen opened her mouth in shock. "I was not! And I'm still not jealous of you. You do stupid things all the time. You made Jake run away with you..."

"Stop right there! I did not make him run away. We went on *rumspringa* and it was his idea." Cassandra lied to make her sister stop saying dreadful things about her. She was tired of her constant taunts.

"I didn't know that."

"There's a lot of things you don't know. Like, I wouldn't be a *gut mudder*—end of story. I'm just gonna do what *Mamm* and *Dat* think I should do. They said that Maud will find someone to give the baby to. I don't know anything about babies and what to do with them. I still haven't figured out what I'm doing in life, and my options would be limited with a baby. I worked with a girl at the restaurant who had a baby by herself and it was too hard for her. I don't want to struggle like that.

Gretchen sighed. "You should've thought of all that before..."

"Get out!" Cassandra yelled.

"Why? I'm trying to help you figure out what to do."

"You weren't; you were being horrible. Anyway, there's

nothing to help me with. I'm going to Maud's. It's just a few months out of my life and then everything will be back to normal."

"What about Jake's parents? Don't you think they would like to know that you're having their son's child?"

Cassandra hadn't even stopped to consider anything like that. "*Nee!* I'm the one who'd have to look after the baby all the time if I keep it, so I figure it's none of their business. It's just sentimental nonsense that you think they should know about the baby."

"Why didn't you go to Jake's funeral?"

"Didn't I tell you to get out?"

"Just answer me that," Gretchen said.

"Why does it matter?"

"He was your boyfriend and you made a baby together. You lived together then he died and you didn't go to his funeral. It just seems cold-hearted and I know that deep down you're kind."

"If you must know, he deserted me. He knew about the baby and didn't care. Then he walked out and left me with bills to pay on top of everything else."

"I can't imagine Jake doing anything like that."

"Well, he did! I told him he had a responsibility to the baby and me. Then he told me I had a responsibility to go back to the community and if I didn't go back he had no responsibility to me whatsoever."

"Really? He said that?"

"He said he'd marry me if I returned to the community."

"Then why didn't you?"

"I wouldn't marry a man who wouldn't stand by me.

And he just walked out on me because I wouldn't go along with what he wanted. I would never marry a man who put me in such a situation."

"Well, weren't you doing the same to him? He didn't want to leave the community—that's the way I heard it."

Cassandra screwed up her face. "Gretchen, I can't explain every little detail to you. For a start, you don't know what you're talking about, and you're annoying me. I don't have the time to tell you everything that happened, but I never got along with him. He would've been the last person I would've married. If I came back to the community and he was still alive, I would've *had* to marry him."

"That's not so. You used to tell me how in love with him you were."

"That's before we went on *rumspringa* together."

"Is that what you call it when you never intended on coming back? It's not a true *rumspringa*."

"No one knows if they'll come back or not when they go on *rumspringa*. That's the whole point of it, but I guess, you're too young to figure things like that out."

"Stop being so mean to me."

"Just go, before I call *Mamm* and tell her you're being mean to me."

Gretchen jumped to her feet. "I thought we might be able to be friends when I saw you back here, but you haven't changed a bit."

"And you haven't changed either."

Gretchen walked out her door.

Wanting to deliver a further jab, Cassandra called after her, "You're the reason I left!"

CHAPTER 5

No weapon that is formed against thee shall prosper; and every tongue that shall rise against thee in judgment thou shalt condemn. This is the heritage of the servants of the LORD, and their righteousness is of me, saith the LORD.
Isaiah 54:17

CASSANDRA SLEPT BETTER that night because she had a plan. But should she go along with what her mother and father said and go to Maud's? It was far enough away that news of a birth wouldn't get back to her community. She would also be away from anyone who would get suspicious when her stomach got bigger.

Still lying in bed, she placed her hands on her stomach. She was starting to swell a little. Cassandra threw back the bedcovers, stretched her arms over her head and sat up.

She slipped on the same dress that she'd had on for a

few hours the day before, stuck on the prayer *kapp,* tied on her apron, and pulled on black stockings before she headed downstairs.

As she approached the kitchen, she heard Gretchen ask, "Will Cassandra be doing chores while she stays here?"

"Nee, I won't be." Cassandra walked further into the room, and sat down at the kitchen table.

Her mother made no comment only glanced at both girls before she turned back to the pancakes she was cooking on the stove.

Gretchen stared at her sister, "It won't hurt you to do a bit around the place here before you go to Maud's."

Cassandra glanced up at her mother.

Gretchen continued, "I already told *Mamm* I heard everything, and I won't tell anyone your secret. But I don't know why people can't know about it."

Their mother turned around from the stove. "You mustn't tell anybody, not even your sisters." Their mother shook a spatula at Gretchen.

"I said I wouldn't."

Cassandra said, "It'll only hurt *Mamm* and *Dat* if you tell anybody. I don't mind about me, but you wouldn't want to hurt them, would you?"

"I already said I wouldn't tell anybody and I meant it."

Cassandra leaned forward and said to Gretchen, "Let's see how long you can keep a secret now that you're older. You could never keep one before."

"Girls stop it! I forgot how peaceful it was without you around, Cassandra."

Cassandra was hurt by her mother's comment and by her sister's smirking face. "It's not me, *Mamm,* it's her."

"I don't care who it is. I just want it to stop. You're both old enough to put this childish behavior behind you."

Gretchen curled her lip into a snarl and Cassandra pulled a face right back at her.

Their mother said, "I wrote a letter last night, and I'm going to put it in today's post. As soon as we hear back from Maud, you should probably make your way there, Cassandra."

"Can I go too?" Gretchen asked.

Her mother swung around from the stove. *"Nee,* that would be the last thing that I would do to poor old Maud. She wouldn't be able to take the two of you together."

"Old? Exactly how old is she?" Cassandra asked, not wanting to have to look after some old lady. Was that the real reason she was being sent there, to be a nursemaid?

"Only a couple of years older than your *vadder."*

"That's ancient," Gretchen said.

"She's not that old, then," Cassandra said, only to disagree with her sister.

Mrs. Yoder put a pile of pancakes in the middle of the table. "Eat up."

"Denke, Mamm," Gretchen said.

"Jah, denke, Mamm," Cassandra said.

"You'll see everyone tonight at the *familye* dinner."

"The what?"

Cassandra's mother sat next to her. "We have dinner with everyone over on Tuesday night."

Cassandra knew that 'everyone' meant her older sisters and their families.

CHAPTER 6

Knowing that whatsoever good thing any man doeth,
the same shall he receive of the Lord, whether he be bond or free.
Ephesians 6:8

"GREAT! What are we going to tell them?" Cassandra asked.

Gretchen smirked. "Why don't you just lie like you usually do?"

"Gretchen, now is not the time for smart talk," Mrs. Yoder said. "We won't say anything to them. It's got nothing to do with them."

"I disagree. It has everything to do with them. They are about to lose their niece or nephew," Gretchen said.

"It's not your decision to make, Gretchen. This is about Cassandra and not about you."

"Just because I'm the youngest, you treat me like a child, and you never listen to me."

"Your opinions do matter, but not on this occasion," Mrs. Yoder said.

Cassandra stared at Gretchen. "You know why I can't have this baby."

"Don't you want to see your sisters?" Mrs. Yoder asked Cassandra.

Cassandra nodded. "I suppose so, but not if they're going to ask me a lot of questions."

Mrs. Yoder frowned. "They will. They haven't seen you in ages. I don't think you can avoid them asking questions."

Gretchen said, "They'll probably ask you why you didn't go to Jake's funeral."

"Nee, they wouldn't talk about Jake. They would worry it would upset Cassandra," Mrs. Yoder said.

Cassandra put her hand to her head. "I feel a headache coming on."

"There's no getting out of it. As soon as your sisters know you're here, they'll want to see you anyway," her mother said. "Just have a rest today. I'll post the letter to your aunt and then I'll come right back."

"I'll go with you, *Mamm,"* Gretchen said.

"Nee, you stay here with your *schweschder."*

Gretchen pulled a face. "Why don't I go post the letter and you stay here?"

Their mother nodded. "Okay, if that's what you want to do. Do you want to go with her, Cassandra?"

"Nee, I'll stay here and think and try to get over this headache."

"I'll go as soon as I eat breakfast. Do you want anything while I'm out, *Mamm?"*

"Nee, denke."

"Neither do I," Cassandra said.

After breakfast, Cassandra helped her mother wash the dishes while her sister posted the letter to Aunt Maud.

"What if she doesn't post the letter?" Cassandra asked.

"Jah, she will. She doesn't want you here." Mrs. Yoder gave a giggle.

"That's true. I forgot about that. She'll be pleased to get rid of me again."

"I don't know why you girls can't get along."

"It's her; it's not me."

"And she'd say exactly the same thing."

Cassandra picked up another dish to dry. "I'll try harder to be nice to her."

"Denke, that would please your *vadder* and me."

When Cassandra placed the dish down, she pressed her hands against her stomach. "Do I look pregnant? They're not going to guess, are they?"

"Nee, you can't tell at all. They won't guess, so don't worry. We'll tell them you need some time to rest after your *rumspringa* and have decided to go to Aunt Maud's."

"I don't know if they'll believe I'd do a thing like that."

"That's what you are doing. They won't question it."

"Okay. I'm glad you and *Dat* are helping me through this. I wouldn't know what to do by myself. I don't have any close friends." She glanced across at her mother and saw her face. Her mother was holding back tears. *"Mamm,* what's wrong?"

"I'm sad, that's all. Sad that this has happened and you'll have to give your *boppli* up."

"You should be happy. You shouldn't see it as a sad thing."

"I suppose you're right. I just can't help thinking that I've done something wrong as a mother for you to end up in this state."

Cassandra's mouth fell open in shock. How could her mother say things like that about her?

Mrs. Yoder shook her head. "I don't know where I went wrong with you."

"Do you want my help with anything else?" Cassandra asked.

Her mother looked at the stack of dry dishes. *"Nee."*

"I'll be in my room, then." Cassandra threw the tea towel down on top of the dry dishes. She walked up the stairs to her room, upset that her mother and father were always disappointed in her.

IN THE MIDDLE of the afternoon, there was a knock on Cassandra's bedroom door. She'd stayed in her bedroom all day keeping away from her mother so she couldn't possibly disappoint her any further.

"Jah?"

"It's just me," Gretchen said.

"Come in."

Gretchen pushed the door open and stuck her head around the door. "Are you coming to help with dinner? There's a ton of vegetables to peel."

"Okay, I'll be down in a minute."

"Gut."

Before Gretchen shut the door, Cassandra said, "What difference will it make if I help you? I'm only one extra person and you and *Mamm* normally do the vegetables yourselves anyway."

"So, does that mean you're coming to help us, or not?"

"I don't know. I'll think about it for awhile."

Gretchen took a step further into Cassandra's room and placed her hands firmly on her hips. "You haven't changed. You're just as selfish as ever. Just as well you're giving the *boppli* away because you'd be a rotten *mudder."*

"That's a dreadful thing to say, Gretchen. Wait 'till I tell *Mamm* what you just said to me."

"Now you're a turtle tattler as well!"

Cassandra stuck her nose in the air. "I think it's called a 'tittle tattler,' which means a gossiper—and that's not me, it's you."

"Jah, well you would know. You're just as selfish as ever." Gretchen abruptly turned and walked out the door.

Cassandra called after her. "I'm not going to help and if *Mamm* asks why, I'm telling her you're the reason."

Cassandra had felt miserable all day and had nibbled her fingernails right down to nothing. She was worried about too many things. She was concerned that Maud and she wouldn't get along. And what if she couldn't find good parents for the baby? She wasn't going to let just anybody take her baby away. It would have to be somebody really deserving of the child. Maybe a couple who had been desperate to have a child for years and years after they'd found out they couldn't have one themselves.

Half an hour later, boredom led Cassandra to join her sister and her mother in the kitchen.

"There you are at last," her mother said. "Would you mind setting the table and the children's table?”

"I don't mind at all. How many are we setting the table for?”

“There’ll be sixteen adults and eight children. The two babies aren't old enough to sit down yet."

"They certainly know how to breed, " Cassandra murmured. Cassandra set about getting the dishes onto the table, pleased that all the vegetables had been peeled already. If there was one thing she detested, it was peeling vegetables. Most every time she was anywhere near a knife she ended up cutting a finger.

Cassandra had become accustomed to living on take-out, or things that were pre-prepared.

When they heard a buggy, Gretchen rushed to the kitchen window. “It's Flora and Amos," she announced.

"I'll go out to see them." Cassandra hurried out of the house even though she hadn't finished setting the tables.

Her eldest sister, Flora, screamed when she saw her, and rushed to hug Cassandra. "I didn't think you would ever be back. Are you staying for good?"

"I think so. I'm going to visit Aunt Maud for some time."

Her sister took a step back. “Aunt Maud?”

On seeing the look on her sister’s face, her stomach immediately lurched. *"Jah.* Why what's wrong with her? Is she horrid?"

Her sister shook her head vigorously *"Nee,* she’s a very nice person.” Her sister smiled and placed an arm around her shoulders. "Come and see how the two little ones have grown, and you haven't seen my *boppli* yet."

"Hello, Cassandra. It's good to see you."

Cassandra looked up to see Amos, Flora's handsome husband. Flora and Amos had always been so happy together and Cassandra had thought that she and Jake would've had a marriage just like theirs, but now, all hopes of her having a happy marriage were dashed. Once she found a home for her baby, she could have a fresh start in life.

"Hello. It's good to see you too, Amos." Cassandra greeted the boys as Amos lifted each one out of the buggy. They'd grown into mini versions of Amos.

Then her sister pulled the basket out of the buggy. "This is Amelia."

Cassandra stepped forward and peeped into the basket at the sleeping baby. She had a sweet little face with tiny pink lips. "She's as pretty as a picture."

"It was nice to have a girl after two boys."

"I wouldn't know what to do with a baby, but I guess something like that is too far away for me to think about."

"One thing I can tell you as your older *schweschder* is that it's good to have a baby when you're ready to have one and not before. It's a lot of work, and it's a lot of work especially if you're by yourself."

Cassandra looked up at her, shocked. Flora's words cut through the air. It was as though her older sister knew, but she couldn't know—there was no way. She didn't have a large stomach and was still able to squeeze into jeans, so no one would be able to tell in her large Amish dress.

Soon after that her other sisters and their families

arrived. Everyone was just as pleased to see Cassandra as Flora and Amos had been. The house was loud, noisy, and full of people. It was good to see everybody, but Cassandra had soon had enough and just wanted them all to go home.

CHAPTER 7

For we wrestle not against flesh and blood,
but against principalities, against powers,
against the rulers of the darkness of this world,
against spiritual wickedness in high places.
Ephesians 6:12

None of Cassandra's sisters had been surprised to hear that she was going to stay with their Aunt Maud.

It was ten days later when the reply came from Aunt Maud. She said she would be more than happy for Cassandra to stay. A plan was put into place, and two days after Maud's letter, Cassandra was on the train to Aunt Maud and Uncle Max's place. The letter had stated that Uncle Max was picking her up from the train station and together they would travel by bus back to the farm.

When Cassandra got off the train, the only Amish man standing there had to be her uncle. She walked up to him while he was looking everywhere in the crowd but in her direction. "Uncle Max?"

He turned and when he saw her he smiled. "You must be Cassandra."

She smiled back and nodded, pleased to see a friendly face.

"I haven't seen you since you were this high." He held his hand three feet off the ground.

"Has it been that long?"

Uncle Max went on to tell her how many times he and Maud had visited her parents. Most of those times were before she was born. All Cassandra wanted to do was get to where she was going; she didn't want to listen to a lot of talk just to be polite, but she had no other choice.

"I'm sure you're not interested. You look tired," he finally said.

"I am, I'm sorry. It's been a long tiring trip."

"We can get the bus out front. Come on." He looked at her bag. "Is this all you have?"

She nodded.

After a two-hour bus ride, they finally arrived at Oakes County.

"Is your farm far away from here?"

"Not very. I just have to find me a phone to call my boarder, and he'll collect us in the buggy." They found a public phone and the phone call was made.

While they were on the sidewalk waiting for Uncle Max's boarder, Cassandra asked, "So, I won't be the only one staying with you?"

"We have a young man who works his way around the place, but don't worry, he won't get in your way. He stays in the *grossdaddi haus* and you'll be in the main *haus* with Maud and me."

"It's so lovely of you to have me stay, and so kind of you to go to all that trouble of meeting me and bringing me back on the bus. It's an awful lot of trouble for you."

He laughed. "I know what it's like when you're not used to traveling. It can be difficult to find your way around."

"And I suppose you know the reason why I'm staying?"

He nodded. "Yes I do, but you're not the first young lady this has happened to and I'm sure you won't be the last."

"I never thought it would happen to me. I mean, I hear things like this all the time."

"Don't you worry about a thing. Maud will help you sort everything out."

It sounded to Cassandra like Maud might have had many young girls come and stay with her. "Did my older *schweschder,* Flora, ever come to stay with you and Maud?"

His face contorted and he looked away from her. "That's something you might have to ask Flora."

I knew it. She wasn't old enough to remember much about her sister before she married Amos, but she did remember enough to know that Amos and Flora had met and married quickly. Two years after that, they'd had their first child. So if Flora had accidentally got pregnant, where was the baby? She must've given the baby up for adoption. That's why her sister's face had gone so funny when she'd heard Cassandra was leaving to stay with Maud. And if Cassie knew Flora's secret, that meant Flora knew hers, too. Now two of her sisters knew.

"*Jah,* I will be having a talk with Flora."

When the buggy arrived, it was Aunt Maud who was driving and not their boarder. Maud was just how Cassandra had pictured her. She was a shorter fatter feminine version of her father, and just like Cassandra's father, Maud had a ready smile. Cassandra looked at Maud's hair that was poking out from under the front of her *kapp.* The thing that pleased Cassandra most about Maud was that her graying hair had once been dark just like her own. Most of the hair was now gray, but the rest of it was definitely dark.

"Where's our boy?" Uncle Max asked Maud.

"I told him I would come and collect you. I was anxious to see Cassandra as soon as I could." Maud got down from the buggy and gave Cassandra a warm hug.

Cassandra immediately relaxed. She knew she was in good hands with these two. Uncle Max took over driving, and Cassandra chatted with Aunt Maud during the ride. When they got back to the house, all Cassandra wanted to do was sleep for a whole day and a whole night.

"You go and have a lie down before dinner. Come on, I'll show you where your room is," Maud said.

The farmhouse was fairly small and built on a single level. There was a *grossdaddi haus* attached which was nearly as big as the main house. Maud continued to lead the way down the hall. She stepped into a room to the left and Cassandra followed her inside.

Maud opened the windows. "I'll let some fresh air in. It'll help you sleep. This room gets the morning sun."

There goes my sleep-in, Cassandra thought. She was only able to sleep in if the room was dark. Now she'd be waking up as soon as the sun came up. "That's good," Cassandra said to be polite.

"We'll talk about things tomorrow, or even the next day—there's no rush. Whenever you feel comfortable. I'll help you plan what to do," Maud said.

"Denke. I appreciate that and I appreciate you letting me stay here. It's very kind of you."

"Fiddlesticks. No need to keep thanking us. We're family and we look after each other."

Cassandra sat on the bed.

"I'll close the door and let you have a rest."

"Thank you, Aunt Maud."

As soon as Maud closed the door, Cassandra lay back on the bed and closed her eyes.

CHAPTER 8

But I say unto you, Love your enemies,
bless them that curse you, do good to them that hate you,
and pray for them which despitefully use you, and persecute you;
Matthew 5:44

BEEF AND CABBAGE casserole was on the menu for dinner. At least that's what it smelled like from Cassandra's room. Cabbage was something that Cassandra hadn't had in a long time—since before she left on *rumspringa.*

She got out of bed, guessing she had a bit of time before Maud knocked on the door telling her that dinner was ready. She unpacked her clothes from her bag and put them in the chest of drawers. Then she hung her dresses on the clothes pegs by the door.

"Dinner is nearly ready, Cassandra," Maud said through the closed door.

"Denke. I'm awake. I'll be there soon." Cassandra straightened her hair, and then put on and laced up her boots. She walked into the kitchen and stopped abruptly when she saw a man she didn't know sitting down at the kitchen table. He looked up at her and smiled and she stood still.

There was something different about this man. He was ruggedly handsome. He ran a large hand through his dark hair as he stood up. It was then that she saw he had a dimple in his right cheek and a slight one in his chin. She took a step forward knowing that this must be the mysterious boarder who was staying in the *grossdaddi haus.*

"I'm Reuben Scholl."

Cassandra cleared her throat and it took her a moment to find her voice. "I'm Cassandra Yoder."

"It's nice to meet you, Cassandra Yoder. I hear you're staying here for a time on vacation."

"Jah, I am."

"Perhaps you might like someone to show you around while you're here? If it's alright with your Aunt Maud, would you like me to show you around tomorrow afternoon?"

"I would like that very much. Is that alright with you, Aunt Maud?" Cassandra looked over at Maud, who was serving the food into large tureens.

"If that's what you want to do, Cassandra. If that's what you think is best."

Cassandra glanced at Reuben and she could see that Reuben also thought that was a strange response for her aunt to make. Maud could see there was an attraction between the pair and she didn't like it—that was clear.

"I won't go if there's something you want me to do here," Cassandra said to her aunt.

"We need to have a good talk, you and I, Cassandra, but we can do that tomorrow morning." Maud swung around from the stove. "Aren't you going to be too busy with all your building work, Reuben?"

Reuben pulled his mouth to one side as his eyebrows shot up.

It was obvious to Cassandra that Reuben had taken a liking to her, and Maud had most certainly noticed. It was bad timing to meet a man such as this one when she was in her present condition. Although she didn't know anything about the man, she was very interested to find out."

"I can't work the whole time and if I work quickly, I'm sure I'll have time to entertain our guest." He smiled at Cassandra, then looked at Maud, and added, "By working quickly, the quality of my work won't suffer."

Maud nodded. "Okay."

He stared back at Cassandra and she gave a little giggle. She had never been one to do a girly giggle, but there was something about the way he looked at her that made her want to giggle. He made her feel tingly all over.

"You'd better sit down, Cassandra, or Reuben will be standing up forever," Maud said.

"Oh, please sit." She sat down at the table across from him.

"Dinner is not quite ready. It'll be another ten minutes or so. We're waiting on your Uncle."

"That's fine," Cassandra said. Hoping to impress

Reuben, she added, "Aunt Maud, can I help you with anything there?"

"Not on your first day here. Perhaps you can help me tomorrow."

"I'd love to." Cassandra flashed Reuben a big smile and Reuben was still staring at her. It seemed he could not take his eyes from her.

"Where are you from, Reuben?" she asked.

"All over the place. I left Ohio when I was thirteen and I've been traveling around ever since."

"Like a gypsy?"

He laughed. "I'm not too certain about that. I travel here and there and do work for people. I'm staying here helping your aunt and uncle rebuild their barn, and when I finish I'm sure something else will come up. Usually, when I finish one job, another is offered to me."

"The Lord provides," said Maud listening into their conversation.

"And what kind of work do you do, Cassandra?" Reuben asked.

"I've come back from *rumspringa* only weeks ago and I was working part time as a waitress."

"Did you enjoy that?"

"Sometimes yes and sometimes no. At any rate, it helped pay the bills."

"How long do you think you'll be staying here?"

"A good few months I'd say."

"Will you be looking for a job while you're here?"

She opened her mouth to speak, but didn't know how to answer. She could probably have a part-time job or even a full-time job for a few months. That would give her something to do instead of hanging around the house. "I suppose I could. I haven't really thought things through."

Reuben leaned in, and said quietly, "Shall we say around two o'clock tomorrow?"

"That sounds good to me." Cassandra nodded.

Uncle Max walked through the back door with his black dog. He ordered his dog to sit down on the mat at the door. His dog sat down and then got up again. "You get back there now." He groused at his dog and his dog looked up at him with big round eyes and slowly walked back to the mat and sat down. Max walked through to the kitchen.

"Ah, we're all here now," Max said.

"*Jah* and we've been waiting on you. Go and get washed up and then I can serve dinner."

"Very good."

Cassandra smiled at that, the way her aunt was bossing her husband around. She looked over at Reuben and they exchanged smiles. It seemed he was amused by their conversation as well.

Cassandra had been right; dinner was beef and cabbage casserole. And just like dinners at home, there were plenty of vegetables to accompany the meal along with fresh bread.

Over dinner, Cassandra learned that Reuben's parents died when he was a youngster and that was the main reason he moved around all the time. He had no proper home.

Reuben heard about Cassandra's family and how she was the second-youngest girl in a large family of girls.

After dinner, Cassandra was quick to offer help to clean the kitchen to impress Reuben. Maud said she could manage and for her to go and sit in the living room in front of the fire with the men. Cassandra had insisted on helping and while the men were in the living room, Cassandra and Maud busied themselves with the washing up.

"He likes you, you know?"

"Reuben does?"

Maud nodded. "*Jah,* he does. He's a good boy. We've known him for some time. He always stays with us when he's got work nearby."

"I'm sensing you want to warn me about him or tell me to stay away from him." Cassandra always thought the straightforward approach was the best.

"I can see there's something between the two of you. I have a knack with these things, and I think it would be best if you tell him early on the real reason you're here."

"If I thought he and I would ever have a serious relationship, I'd tell him. Of course I would."

"You're right. It makes no sense to be telling something like that right now."

"*Jah,* that's right and this is supposed to be secret."

"Secret from people back in your community. You will be going to the meetings here, won't you?"

"I guess I will, but I'll just make myself some bigger dresses. Do you have a sewing machine?"

"*Jah* I do. I'll help you when the time comes. We can cover you up with big dresses and no one will notice."

"*Denke,* that's very kind. I don't think my dressmaking skills are too good; it's been awhile."

They made hot tea and took it to the men.

Again the conversation with Reuben by the fire was easy and flowed naturally.

After a few hours talking, Reuben excused himself and retired to the *grossdaddi haus.* Cassandra considered she better do the right thing so she took the dishes and the teapot into the kitchen, telling Maud that she would do all the washing up.

"I can't have you doing all that the first night you're here. What would your mother say?"

"My *mudder* would say, *'go to bed, Aunt Maud, it won't take long to wash these few things up.'*"

Maud laughed. "Nearly right, but your *mudder* would never call me Aunt Maud."

"She calls you Aunt Maud all the time."

Cassandra laughed as she carried the cups and teapot into the kitchen. As she washed the final few dishes, she heard the muffled voices of Maud and Max. She hoped that Reuben would stick around for many more months. As soon as she put the dishes away, she turned off the overhead gaslight and headed off to bed.

CHAPTER 9

Blessed is the man that endureth temptation:
for when he is tried, he shall receive the crown of life,
which the Lord hath promised to them that love him.
James 1:12

THE SUN STREAMING through her window woke Cassandra bright and early the next morning.

"Dratted sun, " she murmured, as she placed a pillow firmly over her face. It was no use; she was already awake and once she woke up that was it. She could never go back to sleep once she was awake.

Her lips twitched at the corners when she remembered that today she would be spending time alone with Reuben. She could find out more about him and hopefully not tell him too much about herself.

It was only Maud and Cassandra for breakfast as

Uncle Max was already at work and Reuben only had dinner with them.

Cassandra looked down at the scrambled eggs on her plate. "These look delicious *denke. Denke* for getting up so early and cooking."

"I do it every day. It's not any more work to do it for two than it is to cook for one."

"Do you cook when it's just you for breakfast?

"I get up at five in the morning and get Max off to work. He said I don't need to, but I like to start the day with him." Maud smiled and Cassandra could tell she must still be so very much in love with Max to want to be around him so early in the morning.

"Is there *kaffe?"* Cassandra asked.

"Jah, I'll pour you a cup."

"I'll do it."

By the time she'd spoken, Maud was standing at the coffee pot pouring a cup.

Cassandra said, "I like a cup of *kaffe* in the morning. Only one in the morning and the rest of the day I drink tea."

Maud looked across at her. "Should you be drinking *kaffe?"*

"I think so. No one told me not to. I have had one visit to a doctor and that's all. I suppose you have a midwife around here somewhere?"

"I do. She's a *gut* friend of mine. We can go to see her next week."

Cassandra nodded and took hold of the cup that Maud was passing to her. *"Denke."* Cassandra brought the coffee to her lips and breathed in the smell before she took a sip. "Mmm, this is *gut kaffe.*"

"It's quite strong."

"That's the way I like it."

"We'll have to have that talk today. I'll feel better once I have a plan. And

we can start now if you like. There's no one about to hear us."

Cassandra had a mouthful of eggs and all she could do was nod. When she'd swallowed, she said, "That would be good, *denke.*"

"Now, your *mudder* said in her letter that you're looking for a *familye* to adopt your *boppli,* is that right?"

"*Jah.* I would like to find a couple who would be very good at looking after a child. I can barely look after myself," Cassandra joked.

"You wouldn't be the only person ever to bring up a child alone. You learn on the job. Have you considered keeping the child?"

"I can't. What would people think?"

"People think what they will think."

"I know my parents don't want me to do that. They're worried about what people in the community would think and that's why I'm here. I can't return with a baby, I just can't!"

"I respect your parents very much, but this is your life, not theirs. You're the one who has to make the decision and once it's made it can't be unmade. Once you give up rights to your child, you can't change your mind and take the child back."

"Yes, I know that. And I can't see that me ever having a

baby is the right thing for me. Maybe if Jake hadn't died and hadn't run out on me, we could've raised the baby together."

"*Jah,* your *mudder* mentioned that in her letter. I'm sorry to hear what happened to Jake. We must be thankful he'd returned to the community before he died. He's home with *Gott.*"

"We were living together and he chose to return to the community even though I didn't want to. I don't think he even told his parents or anyone that I was having a baby because no one said anything to me." Tears came to her eyes. "He just walked out and left me."

Maud leaned over and patted her arm. "You have to think about yourself now. He's gone and won't be back."

"If his parents do know, maybe they don't want to know. I think the only thing for me is adoption."

"It's a difficult decision and only you can make it. If you do want to keep the baby, you could always stay on here if you feel funny about returning to your parents' community."

Cassandra had never known such kindness. "That's so nice of you to offer that, but I've got no job and no way to support myself." She took a deep breath, and leaned over and pushed her knife into the soft butter and placed lashings of butter onto the fresh bread.

"*Gott* always provides. Sometimes all that is required of us is that we make the first step. Make a decision and take one small step forward, and then *Gott* will direct your next step."

"Sounds so easy when you say it like that. I think the

best thing for me is to find a couple for my *boppli* and *Mamm* said you could help me do that."

"I'll help you. I've done it before for a few girls just like you."

"Including one of my sisters?"

Maud stared at Cassandra, her eyes nearly popping out of her head.

"I'm sorry, you don't have to answer that. I just got an idea that one of my sisters might have been in the same position as me many years ago."

"That's not for you to ask or me to tell," Maud said shaking her head.

"I would like to find a *familye.* How will you do that?"

"I'll ask around. I know a lot of people, and the midwife I told you about is in contact with an agency."

"An adoption agency?"

"Jah."

"I never thought about that."

"These days it's different from what it used to be. You can have no contact with your baby or you can arrange that you see your baby as he or she grows up."

"No contact would be best." Cassandra put her hand around her coffee cup. "I don't know. I'm not sure."

"There's no hurry at the moment. You've got time to make up your mind."

Cassandra nodded. "When do we start?"

"I'll ring Jenny, she's the midwife, and I'll have her come 'round and you can talk with her. That'd be the first thing to do."

"Okay *denke.*"

Cassandra and Maud finished breakfast and cleaned up the kitchen.

"What can I do around here today—this morning, since Reuben is showing me around this afternoon."

"I'll show you around the house, the vegetable garden, and where we keep the chickens. Then we'll get the sewing machine out and see if it's in good working order since I haven't used it for some time. Don't worry, if it's not working Max will be able to repair it. Max can fix anything."

"I'd like that." Cassandra had been hoping that Maud would say there was nothing to do. All she wanted was go to her room and lie in bed until the time came when she could see Reuben.

The morning dragged by, then Cassandra helped Maud make soup for lunch. Max came home for lunch, but there was no sign of Reuben. Cassandra desperately wanted to find out where Reuben went during the day because they had said he was helping build the barn, but he was nowhere near the barn.

CHAPTER 10

Be sober, be vigilant; because your adversary the devil,
as a roaring lion, walketh about,
seeking whom he may devour:
1 Peter 5:8

REUBEN WALKED into the kitchen just as Max was going back out to work. Cassandra had just finished wiping the last dish.

"Are you ready to go?" he asked Cassandra.

Cassandra looked at him and then turned to Maud. "Is there anything else I can do for you before I go with Reuben?"

"*Nee.* You go ahead."

"Before you head off, Reuben, would you like some soup?"

"*Nee, denke,* Maud. I already grabbed something to eat in town."

Cassandra walked to the back door with Reuben. He held the door open for her

"This way, " he said as he nodded toward his wagon.

"Is that your work wagon?"

He smiled. "*Jah.* I don't have a buggy, if that's what you mean. This is what I use to get around.

Cassandra nodded. He helped her up into the wagon. Cassandra was anxious to learn more about him, but she didn't want to sound like she was interrogating him. She had to try to find a way to weave all the questions into the conversation. He climbed up next to her, turned the wagon around and headed out to the road.

"I thought you said at dinner last night that you were fixing the barn, but I didn't see you at the barn today."

He turned to her. "Looking for me, were you?"

She giggled. "*Jah,* I was looking for you. I didn't go to the barn, of course, but I looked out the window wondering where you were." She was relaxed enough around him to know she could say anything and he would think it funny.

He looked at her and arched an eyebrow with his lips turned slightly upward at the corners.

Cassandra said, "You said you were working at the barn, and then you weren't working there, so I was just wondering; that's all."

"Your *ant* and *onkel* bought a farm close by to help some people out. And they've leased it back to the owners. I'm helping the owners—the previous owners—fix the barn. And then I'm going to be helping them do a few small repairs to the house. They are an elderly couple."

"Maud and Max bought their property to help them?"

He nodded. "They won't make a cent. It'll most likely cost them, but they couldn't see the Dawsons' lose the *haus* where they'd raised their *kinner.* Their *kinner* weren't in a position to help, but Maud and Max were."

"That was kind of them."

"You don't know them very well, I'm guessing?"

"*Nee.* I think they only visited once when I was a small child."

"What brings you here to see them, and to come here for such a long stay? Not that I'm complaining mind you. I'm glad you've come here. You're refreshing to have around."

Cassandra smiled. "I'm just back from *rumspringa* and I'm deciding what to do with my life."

"Do you think you might not stay within the community?" He looked at her with concerned eyes.

"*Ach nee.* I will definitely stay in the community." She flashed him a big smile. At this stage, she was telling him anything she thought he wanted to hear. "Anyway, you can't talk. You travel all over the place and don't stay put."

"That's funny. Sometimes we want what we can't, or don't, have. All I want to do is have a place to call home—to put down some roots." He choked up.

Cassandra put her hand on his without thinking. It wasn't because she liked him; she felt true compassion for his sadness. When he glanced down at her hand, she pulled it away, embarrassed.

"I'm sorry."

He smiled. "Don't be."

She cleared her throat. "Where are we going?"

“I'll drive you around the shops where you might find a job. That’ll keep you here longer."

“That’s your plan, is it?”

He smiled. “It is.”

“I’ve only worked in restaurants."

"We have restaurants. The town’s not *that* small. I’ll drive past them and you can see where they are."

"That sounds good."

After they drove past the shops and restaurants in the town, Reuben parked the wagon. “Why don’t we go for a walk?”

“I’d like that. It’s a lovely day for one.”

As Reuben tied the horse to the post, Cassandra thought about Jake towards the end of their relationship. Jake had drawn away from her and they weren't getting along at all. She didn't know whether it was her fault or his; all she knew was that she was mad at him for leaving her alone with the baby. After all, it was just as much his baby as it was hers. Jake leaving her so suddenly had made her vow that she would never marry, or trust another man.

Reuben was confident, manly and independent. Cassandra knew in her heart that Reuben was a man who would never let her down. Surely he was a man who’d stand by his woman no matter what. Maybe she had been wrong to think all men would be the same as Jake.

"Are you ready? Or are you waiting for me to help you down?" Reuben said standing near her.

She smiled and put out her hand. He gave a low chuckle as he stepped forward and took her hand to help her down. Once she had her two feet on the ground, he held onto her hand a little too long before he let it go.

"Let's go this way." He nodded his head in a northerly direction.

As they walked side-by-side, she wondered if he'd ever had a girlfriend. She guessed he was in his mid-twenties so he must've had a girlfriend before now. Why was a man like him unmarried and free to travel around? He must have met a large number of women on his travels.

"I've lived around here most of the time these last few years, and I guess, I feel at home in this community more than anywhere else."

Cassandra appreciated him telling her things about himself. "How many people in the community here? I thought it was pretty small."

"There are about fifty adults, not including the children." He laughed. "There are always plenty of children."

Cassandra knew she wouldn't be one of those women to have a tribe of children. If she got married, she would probably get married late in life—considering this setback she was having. It would be hard for a man to understand the situation she was now in, but it wouldn't be long before Reuben found out the real reason she was here and how would he react?

"We have about three hundred people in our community back home."

"That's a lot. I prefer the smaller communities; that way you get to know people better."

"And that's a good thing? I'm not so sure if I want people to know everything about me."

He laughed and being a good six inches taller than she

was, looked down at her. "And what would you have about yourself that you wouldn't want people to know?"

He'd laughed as though there would be nothing to hide and she was being silly. She couldn't tell him her secret so early. They weren't in a relationship, so there was no reason to tell him.

"Sometimes I just like to keep to myself, that's all," she said.

"Spoken like someone who has never been by themselves I'd say."

"What do you mean?"

"Seems that everybody wants what they don't have. You've grown up with people around you all the time, so you want fewer people around you. I've grown up the opposite, with hardly any people around me, and now I want to have people around me."

"That's true. I wonder why that is. People want the opposite of what they have sometimes."

"I guess it's human nature to want things, because everybody wants something."

"And what is it that you want, Reuben?"

Without hesitating, he replied, "I would like to find a woman to marry and have many *kinner* with."

Cassandra laughed.

He laughed along with her. When he stopped, he asked, "What's so funny?"

"It's just that I have never heard anybody say what they want like that, so openly."

"I didn't know I was supposed to keep things like that a secret."

She raised her eyebrows "I guess it shouldn't be a

secret." She shrugged her shoulders. "I don't know, but you might scare some women away."

He touched his fingers to his broad chest. "Me? Scare someone away?"

She nodded. "It might."

"Isn't that what women want—to get married and have babies?"

"I suppose it is."

"So that's what I've been doing wrong all these years—I've been scaring women away."

She giggled. "Quite possibly."

"Am I scaring you?"

She shook her head. *"Nee."*

"And if I've been scaring women away you must be scaring men away."

He stopped walking. "I'm sorry. I forgot about your boyfriend's death. Forgive me."

"It's okay. We weren't going to get married. The truth is, he left me and went back to the community and told me I had to return as well."

"You didn't want to?"

"I guess I would've come back eventually, but I wasn't ready. I don't think I would've married him."

"That doesn't make his death any less hard on you."

"It was a shock. It was to everybody in the community. I didn't tell you how he died. He was heading for a job interview and stopped by a gas station for a bottle of soda. It was a hot day. There was an armed hold-up, there were shots fired, and he was accidentally shot, killed by a stray bullet."

He lowered his head. "It's a hard thing for you, to go

through such loss at such a young age."

"You've been through loss at a younger age."

"Jah, I guess it's not easy at any age. Even though people say *Gott* wanted them home, or it was all in *Gott's* plan, it doesn't make it easier." He shook his head. "They still aren't there with you."

"Nee, it doesn't. It doesn't make it any easier at all." Cassandra could only imagine how hard it was for Reuben with his parents dying when he was at such a young age, and him being the only child. She'd always taken her family for granted. When she found she was alone and pregnant, there was always home, but what if there hadn't been home? She'd gone home knowing that her parents would have the answers. And they had. They'd sent her to Aunt Maud. What would've become of her if she'd had no one?

Reuben bumped into her shoulder and she looked up into his dark eyes.

"It's time to talk about something else. Important people in our lives have gone and there's nothing we can do about that. I guess I was wrong. It is some comfort that I will see my parents again."

"Jah, I know what you mean. I was just thinking the very same thing."

"We have to make the best of each day."

He smiled at her and all she wanted was for him to wrap his arms around her, but it was too early for that since they'd only just met. Maybe one day something might develop between them; that was what she hoped.

"Jah, we have to make the most of each day. That's true."

CHAPTER 11

Truly my soul waiteth upon God: from him cometh my salvation.
He only is my rock and my salvation;
he is my defence; I shall not be greatly moved.
Psalms 62:1

"What about this restaurant?" Reuben asked when they stopped in front of an Italian restaurant called Michello's.

"It looks nice enough. Have you eaten here before?"

He shook his head. "I'm not one for eating out much."

"You haven't eaten at any of the restaurants around here?"

"Just at the diner up the road. At the end of the street."

She tipped her head to one side. "Haven't you been to a nice restaurant while you've been here?"

He narrowed his eyes at her. "Are you teasing me or something?"

"*Nee,* I'm not. It's my way of finding out why you're not married yet. I'm thinking you haven't even been on a date." He looked away from her. "You haven't, have you?"

He smiled. "You're just trying to delay talk of finding a job."

"*Nee,* I'm not. If I wanted a job so quickly, I'd get a job quickly. I just want to take my time."

"Fair enough." He kept walking and she hurried to keep up with him.

"Why haven't you ever married?" she asked.

"You can't just decide to get married and then marry someone. There has to be someone around at the right time, someone that you want to marry. And who wants to marry you."

"Are you saying that you've never found anybody you wanted to marry?"

"Correct."

"So what sort of woman are you looking for?"

"Who said I'm looking for anybody?"

"You did, just before."

He chuckled, scratched his forehead and stopped walking. "That's right, I did didn't I?"

"*Jah,* you did." Cassandra laughed and he joined in with her laughter.

"I'm looking for a kind and caring someone, easy to talk to, someone soft and with a gentle nature—someone like you."

"Someone like me? You don't even know me."

"I know you well enough to know that you've got all those qualities."

She smiled. "That's nice of you to say."

"I'm not saying it to be nice. There is something very delightful about you."

"Nobody's ever said that about me before."

"Maybe no one has seen what I see." He started walking again.

They came to another restaurant.

"Well, this place has got no end of restaurants," Cassandra said.

"It's fairly easy to get a job around these parts," he said. "Feel like a bite to eat?"

Cassandra said, "I've only just had lunch not long ago."

"Kaffe?"

"I guess I could do with another *kaffe,"* she said, ignoring her one-coffee-a-day rule.

"There's a bakery up here that serves *gut kaffe.* And before you ask, I've been there before, alone."

Cassandra giggled. "I wasn't going to ask that."

They looked into the bakery window.

"I wasn't hungry, but now I am," Cassandra said. "Everything looks good. I might be able to squeeze in a piece of cake."

"Let's go in, shall we?" He took a step to the left and pushed the door open for her, and she walked through.

There were only two tables occupied.

Cassandra turned around and said, "Where would you like to sit?"

"There by the window so we can watch people walk past."

Cassandra gave a little giggle as she sat down at the small table. Everything seemed so normal and natural with Reuben.

A waitress came over and took their coffee orders. "Will that be all?" she asked.

Reuben looked over at Cassandra. "What kind of cake would you like, Cassandra?"

"I'll have a cupcake with pink icing please."

"And I'll have a coffee scroll," Reuben said to the waitress, who gave a hint of a small head nod and walked away.

"You could easily do that," Reuben whispered.

"It's not so easy all the time. Sometimes it's really busy, well, it was where I used to work. I didn't mind being a waitress, but that's the only job I've tried. Maybe I would like to try something else."

"Like what?"

"I don't know yet. I'm still young," she said with a giggle. "I could do anything."

"Exactly how 'young' are you?"

"Is that a question a gentleman should ask a lady?"

"I think it's okay, unless the lady has something to hide."

Cassandra felt her face flush. She did have something to hide, but it wasn't her age. So he wouldn't notice her embarrassment, she quickly added, "I'm turning twenty soon."

He leaned forward. "How soon? Should I be buying a birthday cake instead of a coffee scroll and a pink cupcake?"

Cassandra laughed. "In a few weeks' time."

"We'll definitely have to have a party."

Cassandra shook her head. "I'm not one for parties."

"Spoken like someone who comes from a large *familye.*"

She raised her eyebrows. "Is that what it is?"

"It's nice to have people to celebrate with for things like birthdays, Christmas, and Thanksgiving. I'm often alone at those times. At any rate, I don't tell anyone when my birthday is."

"I didn't ask you."

"Why not?" he asked.

She sighed. "Okay. When's your birthday?"

He laughed. "I happen to share my birthday with Christmas Day."

"Well, that's something that's easy to remember."

"Will you still be here at Christmas time?"

Since the baby was due in March, she'd be there for Christmas. "I plan to be here. Will you still be here?"

"I think there's going to be enough work around here for me to stay until a little after Christmas."

"Well, Christmas will have to be a double celebration."

"I don't want anybody to know."

"Yes you do, or you wouldn't have told me."

He laughed, and the waitress bringing over their cups of coffee interrupted them.

"I'm not used to sharing much about myself," he said as he poured a spoonful of sugar into his coffee.

"I don't like talking about myself either."

"You've done a good job so far. I found out quite a bit about you and your *familye.*"

"That's good."

He looked over her shoulder. "Here come our cakes."

The waitress placed their cakes on the table.

"Thank you," Reuben said.

Cassandra looked down at the icing that was standing tall on the cupcake. It was wound around in a spiral pattern and on top of the icing was a red star. She pulled off the star and looked at it. "I wonder if this is edible."

Reuben leaned over as though to get a closer look. He promptly plucked it from her hand, and popped it into his mouth. *"Jah,* it's edible."

Cassandra laughed. "How could you do that? That was mine."

"She who hesitates is lost. If you snooze, you lose."

"I'll remember that," she said, as she moved her cake a little further away from him. "And I've got a long memory. Just tell me; did it taste good?"

"It was delicious."

She shook her head and poked her fork into the icing while Reuben bit into his coffee scroll.

"The food here is good."

"Well, the icing is good. I haven't started on the cake yet. As for the star—I'll never know."

"Delicious."

She had never had fun like this with Jake. Jake was always way too serious to be a good match for her. When she realized they weren't suited, they were already committed and living together. Things went from bad to worse when she found out she was expecting, and then he abandoned her. Something deep down inside told her that a man like Reuben would never leave her alone like Jake had.

"Tell me some more about yourself," he said.

"I think I've told you everything there is to know."

"So far I know you have a lot of sisters, and all the older ones are married. There's just you and your younger sister who aren't. I know what happened to your boyfriend. I know you went on *rumspringa* and you've recently returned. And you've worked in a restaurant. What else should I know?"

"You should probably know that I'm kind, caring, easy to get along with and..."

He leaned back in the chair with a twinkle in his eyes. She had repeated to him everything she recalled that he'd said he was looking for in a woman. She was being a little bit cheeky and she couldn't help herself. There was something about him that made her speak so boldly.

"Well, that's good to know. It seems like my search is over," he said.

They both laughed.

The rest of the afternoon he took her around the nearby farms showing her where many of the people in the community lived. Then they drove by a creek that had a nearby windmill and a small bridge.

He pointed at the windmill. "That's not used any more. I've always wanted to go and explore it and have a look around." He looked at her. "Would you like to do that another day?"

"I'd love to. But I don't want to keep you from your work."

"I'll make time; don't worry about that. I'll gladly make time for you. Perhaps we could do that Sunday after the meeting?"

"I'd like that." Cassandra counted up the days in her head. Today was Thursday, then there was Friday, then Saturday. She'd only have to fill in two more days until she'd have some time with him again.

He looked over at her and they exchanged smiles. This had to be the man God had found for her. She didn't know how things were going to work and how having the baby would fit in with God's plans. Reuben had said that he wanted a lot of children so he should be pleased that she was already having one. Or would he?

Once Reuben found out about the baby, he'd find out what kind of relationship she'd had with Jake on *rumspringa.* At the moment, he didn't know that they'd shared an apartment, living as man and wife. How would he feel about that? Although *rumspringa* was a time when young people could do anything, before their baptism into the Amish faith, she wasn't so sure that one man could accept another man's child, and accept the fact that the woman he loved had conceived that child out of wedlock.

CHAPTER 12

To every thing there is a season, and a time to every purpose under the heaven: A time to be born, and a time to die; a time to plant,
and a time to pluck up that which is planted;
Ecclesiastes 3:1

CASSANDRA WAS WALKING on air after she said goodbye to Reuben when they arrived back at Maud and Max's house. She walked into the kitchen to see Maud sitting at the table shelling peas.

"Hello. Let me do that." She stood by Maud's shoulder.

"*Nee,* that's alright; I've nearly finished. Dinner is underway, so you sit down and tell me how your day went."

Cassandra sat and told her about the restaurant and how they'd said silly things to one another and about the star that he'd snatched from her. "It was silly, but I enjoyed myself more than any other time I can ever remember. It's been so long since I've been so happy."

"Seems to me you've found a friend."

"*Jah,* I think so."

"Well, think very hard, Cassandra, before that friendship develops into something else, or things could get even more complicated for you."

"I know what you mean. I've been a little wary about that myself."

"I can see he likes you, and he hasn't been like that with any of the young women around these parts, and I've known him for many years."

Cassandra nodded. "I'll be careful."

"I had a visitor here today."

"You did?"

"It was Jenny, the midwife."

"*Ach nee,* I missed her."

"I told her about you and she's coming back to see you on Friday."

"*Gut denke.*" Cassandra realized that she had no money and wondered if her parents had made some arrangement with Maud. "Did my parents say anything about money to you? I don't have any of my own."

"It's all taken care of. They said they don't want you to worry about money. They're handling everything. They're helping out with your stay here and paying for the midwife."

"That's a relief." Cassandra wouldn't have thought too much about that before she'd gone on *rumspringa,* but living by herself in the apartment she'd learned the value of money. She'd find a way to repay her parents. If a serious relationship developed between herself and Reuben, Reuben would be impressed that she was making an effort to pay her parents back. Her parents were likely taking care of her financially because they were worried about their reputations, rather than her well-being, but she was still grateful.

Maybe she should get a job at a restaurant even a couple of days a week. But if she got a job, how was she to get to and from work? The eateries weren't close enough to walk, and she didn't want to rely on anybody to take her and collect her.

"What's for dinner?"

"We've got roasted chicken and roasted vegetables tonight."

"Really? That's my favorite. How about I make something for dessert?"

"What would you like to make for dessert? I haven't got that far yet. We usually just have ice cream and fruit."

"How about a pie? I used to make the best blackberry pies at home."

"We don't have any blackberries. But I do have plenty of preserved peaches."

"Why don't I make a peach pie?"

"I've only got the one oven, but I've got the dinner on early enough that I can keep it warm while the pie cooks."

Maud and Cassandra smiled at each other.

"Wunderbaar!" Cassandra was pleased that she and Maud were getting on well, and she even liked Maud's husband. She'd had concerns that she wouldn't get on with the people she'd been sent to stay with, but her fears had been unfounded.

As she rolled out the pastry for the peach pie, she could only think about Reuben. She was already devel oping feelings for him and she wondered how he felt. He seemed to be attracted to her—as far as she could tell. When the time was right, she'd have to tell him about the baby. And that would prove what kind of man he was he was. A real man would stand by her. If he weren't, he would probably judge her harshly and not be interested in her any more.

Reuben walked into the kitchen just as Cassandra was putting the pie into the oven.

"That's not a pie, is it?"

"Don't get used to it!" Maud said. She looked up at Cassandra from her seat at the kitchen table, and explained, "Max and Reuben don't get pies too often around here."

"Well, that can change while I'm staying here. I love baking pies."

"As long as they taste alright, I don't think any of us will have any objection to you doing just that," Reuben said with a cheeky grin

"I'll just have to see if I can get those blackberries for you from somewhere," Maud said.

Just then, Max came through the door and told his dog to sit on the mat. This time, the dog obeyed. Maud and Cassandra served the dinner.

After the pie was eaten at the end of the meal, everyone voted that Cassandra could bake as many pies as she wished and preferably, daily.

That gave Cassandra the idea—she could bake pies and sell them. That way she could make money. She'd set up a roadside stall; she'd seen one not far from the house that sold honey and jams to passers by. Pies would be perfect to sell from a stall nearby.

She kept that thought to herself, and made a mental note to speak to Maud about it soon. She'd like to find a way to repay her parents and this, it seemed, was the perfect solution. Cassandra only hoped Maud would allow her to use her kitchen.

After the dinner clean-up, it was tea in the living room. An hour later, Reuben said goodnight and left for the *grossdaddi haus.*

As she'd done the previous night, Cassandra offered to wash the last of the tea and coffee dishes. At home, she would never have done that. Her family had to put up with her, but these people seemed to enjoy her company. Even Uncle Max, who wasn't exactly a proper relative—being her uncle only by marriage—seemed to like having her around.

CHAPTER 13

Thou wilt keep him in perfect peace,
whose mind is stayed on thee:
because he trusteth in thee.
Isaiah 26:3

THE NEXT DAY, Cassandra discussed the idea of making pies and selling them and, to her delight, Maud liked the idea. Maud told her there was a larger oven in the barn, which she'd always planned to install in the house. Now there was a good incentive for Max to install the stove, moving it up on his list of things to be done.

In the first two weeks, they decided to try all different varieties of pies to see which ones would prove most popular.

Friday morning came. She wondered how she would explain Jenny's visit to Reuben. He'd know that Jenny was the community midwife; of course, he would since it was only a small community. But then again, Maud said that she was a friend of hers, so maybe Reuben would think that Jenny was only at the house as a friend of Maud's.

Cassandra was nervous about meeting the midwife. It wasn't so much about meeting the midwife herself, it was the whole thing of actually giving birth to a child and going through the pain of labor. Meeting with Jenny would make it all the more real. She didn't know if she would be able to do it.

This was the first thing in her life she couldn't change her mind about or get out of. She'd had a history of quitting. She'd grown bored with playing softball and quit even though her friends said they needed her to make up the numbers. She'd changed her mind and put a stop to the contract that would buy them an apartment. It was Jake's money, but he'd wanted them to buy it together. She'd done the same when they were just about to sign for a small car. Commitments were a big thing and Cassandra didn't like that feeling of having to do things. Now she was faced with something she couldn't get out of no matter what. She couldn't simply change her mind about having a baby.

Yes, she didn't want to keep this baby, but that wouldn't stop the baby from coming. Cassandra sat on her bed looking straight ahead. For the first time, she realized how stupid she and Jake had been. There was no rewinding the clock, and it didn't matter that the pregnancy had been an accidental one—that didn't change anything.

She was terrified by the idea of childbirth, but even her parents couldn't fix this problem for her. The only way to end the nightmare she was in was to go through with it until the end. The girls she worked with at the restaurant had told her what it was like to give birth. It seemed there was no painless way to get through it.

What if she were one of those women whose labor took days from start to finish? She couldn't imagine being in pain for such a long period of time. To top it all off, there was no man to hold her hand throughout the ordeal. Jake at least might have been useful for that.

The sound of a buggy outside distracted Cassandra from her worries. She stood up and walked to the window. That had to be Jenny. A youngish woman got out who, Cassandra guessed, must be in her early-to-middle thirties. Cassandra had expected Jenny to be older, closer to Maud's age considering Maud had said that they were friends.

"Cassandra," Maud called from downstairs.

"I'm coming," Cassandra called back. Cassandra took a huge gulp of air and walked downstairs.

She waited at the door with Maud while Jenny secured her white and brown horse. She could see Jenny's face; she looked to be a friendly kind of person, and that calmed Cassandra's nerves somewhat.

"You must be Cassandra," Jenny said as she headed to them.

"Good guess," Cassandra replied with a smile. "That's what my parents named me."

Jenny gave a little laugh and then greeted Maud. Then the three of them walked inside the house.

"What will we do first?" Maud asked.

"Shall we have a cup of tea and talk?" Jenny suggested.

"Come into the kitchen and we'll have a cuppa," Maud said leading the way.

"That sounds nice, and then Cassandra and I will get down to the reason I'm here."

"Gut!" Cassandra said, thinking that it did not sound good at all. What would sound good is if someone could reverse time and take her back to before she left the community with Jake. She would certainly do many things differently if she could have that period of time over again, knowing what she now knew.

"You both sit and I'll get the tea," Cassandra said, being too nervous to sit down.

"So, you haven't been here long, Cassandra?"

"I've only been here a couple of days."

"And how do you like it so far?"

"I like it fine. Oaks County is such a pretty place. Reuben has shown me around." She looked over at Jenny. "Do you know Reuben?"

"Jah, I do. Everyone around here knows him. He's been visiting the community on and off for years."

Cassandra nodded.

"Jah, the two of them have struck up quite a friendship," Maud said.

Cassandra glanced at Jenny just in time to see Jenny smile.

"Is that right?" Jenny said looking across the table at Maud.

Maud nodded and gave a knowing smile.

While she waited for the pot to boil, Cassandra sat down at the kitchen table and said, "I don't mind telling you I'm scared out of my mind."

Jenny nodded. "Most women in your situation are scared. It's only normal."

"That doesn't really make me feel much better."

"It's normal to be nervous, especially the first time, but remember that birthing is a natural process."

"And a painful one?" Cassandra hoped Jenny would tell her there was nothing to worry about.

"There will be a certain amount of discomfort and I won't say that there won't be. The thing is not to talk to too many women about it. You'll get your share of horror stories—there are plenty of those around. But bad experiences are generally in the minority."

"I've heard someone had a labor last for three days. Now I can't get that out of my head."

"Don't let people's stories scare you. It doesn't mean yours is going to be three days, or that you'll have any complications."

"I can have complications? Like what?" Cassandra felt immediately sick in the stomach. "I haven't had morning sickness yet; do you think this is morning sickness? I feel sick in the tummy."

"If you haven't had morning sickness before now, I would say this would be nerves."

"Cassandra, you have to calm yourself down," Maud said firmly.

Cassandra leaned back in the chair.

"I'll make the tea, Cassandra, you sit there and speak with Jenny."

Cassandra didn't reply, she just stared at Jenny. "I just want to know how bad it will be."

"There's no way to know that. Most everybody has a different experience."

"Have you had a baby yourself?"

"*Jah,* I have had three."

"And how was that?"

"Mine lasted between eight to twelve hours but only two to three of those hours were what I would call painful."

"Three hours of pain? I don't know how I can do it."

"It's helpful if you don't see it as though the pain is something attacking you. The pain is useful to you. The pain is opening the way for your baby to get out. And believe me, by the time your baby is due, you well and truly will welcome the discomfort because you're just going to want your baby to be out."

Maud giggled. "Ain't that the truth?"

Cassandra frowned at Maud.

"So I don't see it as pain, I see it is something that I have to go through to get my baby out?"

"Well, that helped me. I just saw the discomfort as something my body had to do to open up. After all, that's what the pain is doing—opening up the cervix to allow your baby to move through."

Cassandra sighed loudly. "And then it will be over?"

"Jah."

"Did Maud tell you that I want to find a nice couple to take the baby?"

"Maud and I discussed that briefly. I'll look into that for you."

"You would? I would feel much better with that sorted out soon."

"I can line up some couples for you to interview. Would you like that?"

"I get to interview them?"

"You can choose the couple. But normally, it's best to wait until you're further along because if you change your mind and want to keep the baby, the couples will be disappointed."

"I can't keep the baby because…." In mid sentence, she thought about Reuben. If she and Reuben fell in love and got married, perhaps they could keep the baby. "Well, maybe it might be a good idea to wait a couple months."

"Okay, we'll do that, then," Jenny said.

Maud placed cups of tea in front of them.

After they'd had tea and cookies, Jenny looked Cassandra over in the privacy of her bedroom. Her blood pressure was taken and Jenny pressed down on her stomach.

"Is the baby the right size?"

"*Jah,* he comes up to here." She touched Cassandra's tummy. "This is the baby's right level for how many weeks you are, and your blood pressure is fine. Do you want to listen to the baby's heartbeat?"

"*Jah,* of course I do. How do you do that?"

"I've got this little machine." She pulled out another contraption from her bag. It looked similar to the blood pressure machine. "This will allow us to hear your baby's heart. It'll be a lot faster than your own so don't panic when you hear it."

"I won't." Cassandra was amazed and pleased that she would hear a sound of life from her baby. Before long she heard a rhythmic swishing sound. "Is that it?"

"It certainly is and he sounds strong and healthy."

"He?"

Jenny laughed. "I call them all 'he' before they're born."

Cassandra was reminded of how her mother was upset with her for calling the baby 'it.' "That's a relief, that he's healthy."

"Do you have any health issues?"

"*Nee,* and I never get sick. Even when people get colds and flu around me, I never catch anything."

"That's good."

"How often will you visit?"

"I won't need to see you for another four weeks. Other than that, I guess I'll see you at the meetings every second Sunday."

"*Jah,* I'll be there."

"Well, that's all we need to do today."

"Denke."

Jenny nodded and helped Cassandra sit up, and then repacked her equipment into her bag. Then they walked back down the stairs to talk with Maud, who was sitting in the living room.

"She's healthy, and the baby is healthy too," Jenny announced.

"I knew that," Maud said, looking pleased.

Cassandra and Maud watched from the porch as Jenny drove away in her buggy.

"Do you feel better now?" Maud asked.

"I feel a lot better. She made me feel at ease. I'm still a little nervous, but she'll be there during the whole birthing procedure, won't she?"

"She will. Would you like me to be there too?"

"Would you please?"

Maud laughed. "Of course I will, if you want me to."

"Jah, please. I would be so happy if you'd stay with me. It'd be like having *Mamm* there." Tears came to Cassandra's eyes and she quickly wiped them away before Maud could see them. For the first time in a long time, she missed her mother. Why wasn't her mother there with her? Didn't she care that she was about to go through something dreadful? The least her mother could do was to be there with her instead of sending her away to some faraway place, to a relative she'd only met once as a young girl.

Maud stroked her on the shoulder. "I'll be your stand-in *mudder."*

Cassandra nodded. *"Denke,* I'm going to need one of those." Cassandra thought it was probably the pregnancy hormones making her so emotional. Either that, or it was the fear of what she would soon have to face.

CHAPTER 14

Praying always with all prayer and supplication in the Spirit, and watching thereunto with all perseverance and supplication for all saints;
Ephesians 6:18

SUNDAY MORNING CAME, and Cassandra made sure she was up bright and early. And it wasn't hard to wake up early with the sun streaming in the bedroom window. She went downstairs and, as Maud had told her the night before, there was only cereal for breakfast because it was a Sunday morning.

"We're leaving in ten minutes," was the first thing that Max said to her.

"I'm ready to go. I just need some breakfast and *kaffe.* That'll take less than ten minutes."

"Maud's upstairs getting ready. She's already had something to eat."

"Okay," Cassandra said to Max. When Max left the room, she poured the hot coffee out of the pot and looked out the window just in time to see Reuben heading down the road in his wagon. *That might be because he said he'd show me around after the meeting.*

Max walked back into the room. "Is there enough *kaffe* left for me to have another cup?"

"Jah, I'll pour you one." Cassandra thought she'd better tell Max her plans for the day. "Reuben is showing me around after the meeting today."

Max sat down at the table. "Didn't he show you around the other day?"

Cassandra nodded and passed him a cup of coffee. "Is there a problem?"

Maud appeared at the door in time to have her say. "Not at all, but he'll be here for a long time and he'll be here when you give birth, so if you're getting close to him, it might be good idea to tell him soon."

"Jah, I know, Maud." Cassandra had already had this conversation with Maud.

"Gut!" Max said.

"Tell me how this is supposed to work, Maud." Cassandra sat down at the kitchen table. "Is this a secret to everyone in the community including the bishop?"

"The bishop will want to speak with you, and when you go to see him, it'll be best to tell him the reason you're here. That doesn't mean that anybody else has to know. Except Reuben—if your relationship develops into a serious one."

Cassandra nodded. "Got it."

Max added, "Once the wrong person finds out, news will travel through the community like wildfire."

"I wouldn't want that," Cassandra said.

"*Nee.* Neither would your parents."

"*Jah.*" Cassandra nodded, not happy about her parents being mentioned.

Maud walked out of the room while Max stood up. He walked toward the back door.

Cassandra grew angry. This was happening to her, not her parents. It seemed selfish of her parents to be concerned about themselves when it was happening to her and not them. She was the one who had to go through the labor and the pain of giving birth, while they were hundreds of miles away enjoying themselves.

"As long as my parents are happy," Cassandra said, as Max was on his way out the door.

He stepped back through the door. "Did you just say something?"

Cassandra shook her head. "It doesn't matter." It certainly didn't matter to her parents.

AS THEY TRAVELED to the meeting, Cassandra was told that the gathering this fortnight would be held at the bishop's house. The Sunday meetings, as in Cassandra's community, were held every second Sunday. Now there was probably no way that Cassandra could get out of talking to the bishop if the meeting was held in his house.

They traveled about five miles and came to a street of houses near the edge of the township.

"The bishop lives in that cream-colored house there," Maud pointed to a house just before Max pulled into its driveway.

There were already about twenty buggies lined up in a row and from the number of people Reuben had told her were in the community that might mean that everybody was already there. They pulled up next to Reuben's wagon and Cassandra noticed that he was nowhere in sight.

She looked over at the house and saw people going inside. She wasn't nervous about meeting new people like she would've been when she was younger. In the back of her mind, the birth was the worst thing she could think that she'd ever have to go through, so meeting new people was nothing in comparison.

Maud got out of the buggy while Max secured the horse.

"We won't wait for Max. The bishop doesn't like people to be late," Maud told Cassandra.

"I'm right behind you."

Maud linked her arm through Cassandra's. "Don't be scared."

"I'm not. Why would I be?"

Maud gave a small laugh. "There's no reason. I just thought you might be."

The bishop's house was much smaller than the typical houses back home. And there weren't many people in the house, which was just as well. The main room in the bishop's house definitely wouldn't have held all the people in her own community.

A few people came up to introduce themselves, and

then everyone took their seats when a man stood up to open with prayer.

"He's the deacon," Maud whispered as she pulled Cassandra into the second front row with her.

As soon as the prayer was over, a man stood up and sang.

"That's Bishop John over there," Maud whispered.

He was a man who appeared to be in his early sixties, with thick hair and beard—a mixture of gray and black.

The bishop gave the word on giving thanks and how we should give thanks every day no matter if we think what has happened to us is bad or good. Cassandra thought that notion quite silly.

Why would she thank God for being in the situation she was in? It wasn't a situation to be proud of or happy about. Having a baby out of wedlock would be the worst thing that could happen to a young woman who was supposed to be Godly.

Maybe the bishop had meant that people could give thanks to God for most of their situations, but certainly not all. That was something she'd find out from him if he wanted to speak with her sometime. She had yet to make the decision to be baptized and become a proper member of the community. As it was, she knew she had one foot in and one foot out. Had it not been for the pregnancy she wouldn't have gone back to her parents' house.

The rest of the meeting was pretty much the same as meetings back home, singing and prayers.

When the meeting was over, she looked over to the other side of the room where the men sat. She caught

Reuben's eye, and he smiled at her. She gave a quick smile back and then looked away.

She knew it wouldn't be good to act too friendly with him in front of other people—tongues would wag. Besides that, if she told the bishop her secret it wouldn't be good if he knew she was becoming close to Reuben.

Everyone moved out of the house.

"We're eating outside today because the weather is fine," Maud said.

Before long, the tables were spread with a huge variety of food.

"There aren't as many people as my community, but there's nearly as much food here," Cassandra said.

Just as Cassandra had suspected he would, the bishop came to speak with her during the meal. Thankfully, there was nobody close by.

"Cassandra, is it?"

"Jah, it's nice to meet you." Cassandra put out her hand and the bishop shook it.

"I know your parents."

"You do?"

"I do. I haven't seen them for many years, but I stayed in their community when I was quite young."

"They didn't mention they knew you, but I guess I didn't ask."

"Would you like to visit with me and my wife—say on Tuesday afternoon?"

"Jah, I would love to. Would you like me to come by myself or would you like Maud to come too?"

"By yourself; that would be preferable."

"All right. I'll have to arrange someone to get me there."

"Let me know if you have difficulty and my wife and I can collect you and bring you back."

"Denke. I should be able to arrange something."

She was certain that Max would take her there and bring her back if the bishop had asked to see her.

When the meal was over, Cassandra, Max, Maud, and Reuben were the last to leave.

"We might as well go from here rather than go back to the house," Reuben said to Cassandra.

"That's fine with me." Cassandra hoped the bishop and his wife wouldn't see the two of them together. She didn't want to have to drop the bombshell that she was pregnant and have to explain her friendship with Reuben all at the same time.

When she climbed up into the wagon, she looked around and the bishop and his wife were nowhere to be seen. She waved goodbye to Max and Maud and then they were on their way.

"What did you think about our meeting?" he asked.

"Pretty much the same as the meetings back home."

"Is that good or bad?"

"Neither good nor bad. It's just that's what I had expected, I guess."

"You don't give much away do you?"

She glanced over to see him smiling. "What do you mean? What would you have me say?"

"Normally people like what our bishop has to say."

"Jah, I did. Put it this way; it certainly got me thinking."

He took his eyes off her and looked back at the road.

She knew she would have to change the subject otherwise they would be talking about the bishop all day and the merits of his sermon.

"And where are you taking me to date?" She laughed. "I mean, today?"

He laughed along with her. "On our 'date,' I'm taking you back to the windmill we saw from the wagon the other day. Remember I told you I wanted to explore around it?"

"I remember. That sounds *gut.*"

CHAPTER 15

Praying always with all prayer and supplication in the Spirit, and watching thereunto with all perseverance and supplication for all saints;
Ephesians 6:18

"I SAW you talking with Bishop John," Reuben said.

"Jah, he seems very nice and his wife does too. What's her name again?"

"Her name is Ruth."

"The bishop asked me to visit them on Tuesday afternoon."

Reuben gave a little chuckle.

"What's so funny? Isn't that what he does with all the people who visit the community?"

"I'm not certain about that. Let me know what happens." Reuben laughed some more.

"Why are you laughing? What's going to happen?"

"I'm sorry. I shouldn't find it funny. I can just picture you there, sipping tea and nibbling very politely on a cookie."

"Jah, that's how it will be because I *am* very polite."

"You're different, that's what you are."

Cassandra pouted not knowing if that was good or bad. "How so?"

"You're different from the other girls."

"I hope that's a good thing."

"It is a good thing. I think it's good to be different. Everybody needs to be their own person."

"Are you giving me a compliment?"

"Jah I am."

Cassandra couldn't stop smiling when she was around him and she hoped he felt the same. "What about you?"

He glanced over at her. "What about me—what?"

"Did you have to talk with the bishop when you first came here?"

He shook his head. "When I first came here, there was an old bishop here. He's since died, and I didn't have to see him either."

"Where is this windmill?"

"Aren't you enjoying this ride with me in the sunshine?"

She giggled. "I am, but the wagon's a little rougher than a buggy."

"Next time I take you out somewhere, I'll arrange to borrow Max's buggy."

"So you're confident there will be a next time?" She lifted her chin and stared at him down her nose.

He grinned. "I'm saying I want there to be a next time,

but I can't speak for you. I think I've got my work cut out for me. I'll have to work very hard to impress you today so you'll go out with me again sometime this week."

"This week. Isn't that moving a little too quickly?"

"You know what I always say?" He smiled at her.

"You snooze you lose?"

He gave a nod. "You're a fast learner."

Maybe the bishop had been right after all. If she had not gotten pregnant, she wouldn't have been sent to Oakes County, to Aunt Maud's. And if she hadn't come to Aunt Maud's she wouldn't have met Reuben. She was sure she would never meet another man as good as he. They rode in the wagon in silence enjoying the sunshine for another five minutes before the windmill came into view.

"Are we here already?" Cassandra asked.

"Yes, here it is," he said, bringing the horse to a halt. He hurried around to help her out of the wagon.

When she stepped down, she said, "You're a true gentleman."

"I am. And that's just one of the many good things about me."

"And what are some other good things about you?"

"I have to leave some things for you to discover by yourself. If I were to tell you everything you would think of me as prideful."

Cassandra laughed. "I was starting to think that anyway."

They walked side by side to the windmill.

"I think this is a very romantic place," he said.

"I don't know about romantic, but it certainly is mysterious."

When they got closer, Reuben said, "There's the door. Shall we go inside?"

"There is no way I'm going inside. It's probably full of spiders."

"And you're scared of spiders?"

"Isn't everybody?"

He shook his head. *"Nee.* Not especially. They keep some smaller pests out of the *haus."*

"You can go inside there if you want and I'll wait out here. If you scream, I'm not coming in there to save you."

He looked at her and pushed out his bottom lip. "I thought you would rescue me."

"Not at all."

He laughed. "Okay; we won't go inside. Let's go for a walk down by the river."

"That I can handle."

As they walked, he said, "I never thought I'd meet a girl like you."

She knew that he was falling as hard for her as she was for him. Was now the right time to tell him the real reason why she was there? She looked up at the sky to see the white fluffy clouds moving steadily along in the cool breeze. It made sense not to tell him now. It would be too easy for him to walk away, but if he just got to know her a little better, then he might truly fall in love with her and stand by her.

Cassandra made the decision then and there to wait and tell him later. Besides, it was still early on in her pregnancy. There were a few months to go before she would even look pregnant and even then no one would be able to tell under the huge dresses that Maud had promised to help her sew.

"I'm sorry, I shouldn't have said anything. It's far too early considering how your boyfriend died recently. It was selfish of me not to think of that."

She nodded. *"Jah.* It is a bit too early to think about things like that."

"Let's just enjoy one another's company," he suggested.

"Jah, I'd like that."

They walked along the banks of the river and exchanged stories about their childhood memories. Reuben spoke a little about his parents, and she told him a little of what it was like while she was living on *rumspringa* away from home and her community. Reuben had never been on a *rumspringa.*

"HOW DID you and Reuben enjoy your time together?"

"We had a really good time. We went for a long walk by the river and it was near an old windmill. He wanted to go inside, but I was scared it would be full of spiders." Cassandra laughed. Then she looked up, wondering why Maud was silent. "Maud, is there something wrong?"

"Nee. It's not my place to say anything. But I wouldn't like to see either of you get hurt and that might be the outcome if the two of you grow close."

"Are you saying I should stop seeing so much of him?"

"Is it going to happen again?" Maud asked with one eyebrow arched.

"He asked me if I would go out with him again during the week."

"And you agreed?"

Cassandra breathed out heavily, and her shoulders slumped as she nodded. "I suppose you're right. That's not the reason I'm here."

"If you and he are meant to work out, *Gott* will work out."

Cassandra wasn't convinced that what Maud said was right, but, nevertheless, she nodded as though she agreed with her.

CHAPTER 16

Commit thy way unto the Lord;
trust also in him; and he shall bring it to pass.
Psalm 37:5

MAUD HAD BEEN RIGHT about everything—Cassandra saw that now. It was the very worst time that she could meet a man like Reuben and under the very worst circumstances. Maybe the bishop would have some answers or was it best not to tell him how she truly felt about Reuben? Perhaps the bishop would think it a little odd that she had feelings for another man so soon. She hadn't been in love with Jake at the end, but she felt she was trapped in the relationship. How would she possibly explain that to the bishop? She had been as good as married to Jake since they were living together as man and wife. Feeling trapped in a relationship would mean nothing to the Amish bishop, who would've only told her to work through the relationship and pray about it. Now that Jake was gone, would the bishop understand what she was going through?

She sat beside Maud at the kitchen table. "What will I do, Maud? I really like him. But I don't know how he'll react when he finds out about the *boppli.* He might think badly of me and he might not want to start off his life with a woman like me."

Maud thought for a while before she answered. "It complicates things. One thing I know is that Reuben is ready to find a *fraa.* He wants to be married. I don't know what to tell you to do other than be careful."

Cassandra sucked in her lips. She didn't get to where she was now by being careful. She was always one to run into things head on without thinking. She knew she had to change. "I had the opportunity to tell him today, but I didn't. It's supposed to be a secret, but can it be from him? He will find out when the *boppli* arrives because he's living so close."

"Nee, he won't. You won't be birthing here in the *haus."*

"Where will I be?"

"That's something you'll have to discuss with Jenny. You'll have the *boppli* somewhere else, maybe in the birthing center at the hospital. From there your baby will go right to whomever you have chosen."

The reality of it all struck Cassandra. The perfect solution to her situation would be if she married Reuben, but that was only if he was happy to raise her baby with her. How was she to know what he would feel about the situation, and whether he would welcome another man's child?

"I certainly didn't come here expecting to have this

problem. In fact, that was the last problem I thought I would have."

"Life's like that sometimes. We never know what *Gott's* got in store for us."

"I wish He'd give me some advance warning next time."

"Don't worry too much about things, Cassandra. Things usually have a way of working themselves out."

"That's what my father says all the time."

"Because that's what *our* father used to say to us." She laughed.

Cassandra didn't know if she'd ever say that to her children because after she gave this one away she didn't know if she'd ever have any more.

"The bishop said he wants me to visit him and his wife on Tuesday afternoon."

"Gut. I'll arrange for Max to drive you there and collect you."

"Would you? That would be *wunderbaar."*

CASSANDRA SAT across from Bishop John in her very best clothes, looking as tidy as she possibly could make herself. She'd polished her black lace-up boots and made sure that every strand of her dark hair was tucked under her prayer *kapp.*

"Do you know why I'm here?" Cassandra asked the bishop and his wife.

"Jah, your parents sent me a letter before you arrived. I know why you're here."

Ruth, the bishop's wife, leaned forward. "And the purpose of your visit."

"That's *gut,* then I don't have to explain it to you."

"Your *vadder* and *mudder* told me that you were on *rumspringa* when..."

Yes, she'd been on *rumspringa,* the time when young-adult Amish people were allowed to live outside the community, if they chose to, and do anything and not be held accountable—it was before the baptism and their official joining with the Amish community. They were allowed a taste of the outside world so they could be clear in their mind whether they wanted to make the commitment and be baptized into the Amish faith.

"Jah, that's right I was—when it all came about. Unfortunately, it's something I can't take back." Cassandra could feel her cheeks were hot. It was embarrassing to sit there admitting what she'd done.

"Have you given much thought to your baptism?" Ruth added, "Would you be baptized now that you've come back to the community?"

Now it was the bishop's turn to speak. "Or are you going back to live life as an *Englischer* after the *boppli* arrives?"

"That's what I'm here to decide."

"You don't know yet?" Ruth asked.

"I'm not certain of anything at the moment."

"We will put no pressure on you. It's your decision to make. Do you have anything you want to talk with us about?" the bishop asked.

"Jah I do. I've been thinking about a lot of things. Is *Gott* punishing me for something? I never got along with

my younger *schweschder* and we're mean to each other sometimes."

Ruth said, "I don't think being mean to your *schweschder* caused your situation."

"I know that, I just mean that..."

The bishop interrupted, "The rain falls on the good and the bad, the just and the unjust."

"Things happen because we're in this sinful world, and there's nothing we can do about that," Ruth said.

"But if you're in the *familye* of *Gott,* you're in this world, but you're not *of* this world."

Cassandra nodded. "What advantage would it be for me to come back into the community and get baptized?"

Ruth's jaw dropped open and Cassandra quickly added, "I didn't mean to offend..."

The bishop smiled and said calmly, "Eternity with *Gott* and your sins will be forgiven and cast as far from you as the east is from the west. You'll be washed clean in the blood of the Lamb."

Ruth seemed to recover from her shock and said, "You'll be a new creature. Old things pass away, and everything will become new."

"That's what I need—a new life."

"We're just here to help you; we're not here to talk you into anything. The decision must be yours. Everybody will have to stand before *Gott* in the Day of Judgment."

"You'll be rewarded," Ruth said, smiling at her before she picked up the teapot and poured a cup of tea. She passed a cup to Cassandra. "Sugar?"

"Nee, denke." Cassandra said to the bishop. "Will you

baptize me here if I want to be baptized before the baby's born?"

"Of course, if that's what you want."

"I'll give it serious thought."

"That's all we can do," the bishop replied. "Besides giving it serious prayer."

CHAPTER 17

Study to shew thyself approved unto God,
a workman that needeth not to be ashamed,
rightly dividing the word of truth.
2 Timothy 2:15

It was around four o'clock when Max brought Cassandra home from the bishop's house. When Cassandra stepped down from the buggy, Max announced he was going right back to work.

Cassandra walked into the kitchen and saw Maud doing dishes.

"Can I help you with anything there, Maud?"

"Nee, I've just finished putting the dinner on, and there'll be no work to do here for another couple of hours until we are ready to have the evening meal."

"Well, that sounds good to me."

"Why don't you go for a walk and enjoy the last of the afternoon sun?"

"I think I might do that. *Denke.* Would you care to join me?"

"Nee, I'll stay here," Maud said.

Cassandra walked away from the house wondering in which direction the property was where Reuben was working.

Now that she'd come to know Reuben she couldn't stop thinking about him and imagining a life with him. A life, one that included her soon-to-be-born child.

She walked for quite a distance and still she couldn't see another house except one in the distance, and there was no sign of Reuben's wagon.

After some time, she made her way back to the house.

Dinner that night was the next time she saw Reuben. She was setting the table when he walked through the back door.

"Hello, you two," he said to Maud and Cassandra, as he walked into the kitchen.

Maud looked up. "Hello there."

Cassandra smiled at him. "Hello."

"I don't think I smell any pies cooking," he said with a cheeky grin.

"I can't bake a pie every night. That would spoil you."

"And what's wrong with being spoiled?"

Cassandra answered, "Being spoiled is being spoiled. Everyone knows that's not good."

When Maud briefly left the room, Reuben said, "Would you like to do something tomorrow afternoon?"

"Don't you have to work?"

He nodded. "I'll wake extra early and work right through so I have some time tomorrow afternoon."

"I'd like that. What will we do?"

"I'll think of something." He flashed her a smile before Maud walked back into the room.

When Cassandra walked to her bedroom that night, she was even more certain that things between her and Reuben were going extremely well. Even Jake and she hadn't gotten along that well at the start. This could be a new life for her—a new life for her and her baby. She placed the kerosene lantern on her nightstand and closed the bedroom door behind her. After she had changed into her nightgown, she untied the strings of her prayer *kapp* and hung it on top of one of her dresses on the clothes peg. She sat on the bed and unwound her hair, freeing it from the braids that had been hidden under her *kapp* all day.

She ran her brush through her long dark hair while looking out the window at the dark night wondering exactly how long it would take for the handsome Reuben to ask her to marry him.

Maud had said he was ready for marriage, and from his own lips he'd said that was what he wanted—to get married and have a family.

Would he be able to forgive her past? That was the only problem she could see that might stop him from taking their relationship further.

THE NEXT MORNING AFTER BREAKFAST, Maud asked, "When are we going to start trying out these pies?"

"Tomorrow? Will tomorrow be all right?

"I guess so. How about we go to the markets today and see what ingredients we can find? We'll see if we can find any blackberries; they should still be in season."

Cassandra breathed out heavily. "Will we get back before this afternoon? I told Reuben I would be able to spend some time with him this afternoon."

"Jah, we should be back by this afternoon."

Maud didn't say anything, but Cassandra could tell Maud was thinking of telling her not to spend so much time with Reuben until he knew the truth. Maud and Max were close to Reuben, so it made sense that they wouldn't want Reuben to get hurt any more than they would want their niece to be hurt.

CHAPTER 18

And thou shalt love the Lord thy God with all thine heart, and with all thy soul, and with all thy might.
Deuteronomy 6:5

THAT AFTERNOON, Cassandra could barely contain her excitement when she heard Reuben's wagon rattling its way up to the house. She hurried out to meet him while trying not to appear too anxious.

"So do you know where we're going yet?" she asked as she climbed up into the wagon.

He smiled at her.

"What is it?" she asked breathlessly.

He nodded to the back of the wagon. She turned her head and saw a basket.

"We're having a picnic?"

Instead of answering her, he picked up a blanket from under his seat and showed her.

She clapped her hands. "I love picnics. I haven't been on one in so long."

"I thought you'd like one," he said as he moved his horse back down the driveway. "And we're going back to ‘our place.'"

"The windmill?" she asked.

"Jah, I figured that should be ‘our place.'"

Cassandra giggled, glad that things were going better than she had ever hoped. No one had ever made her feel so happy or as special as Reuben was making her feel right now.

When they arrived at the windmill, dark clouds were gathering overhead.

"I hope it's not going to rain for our picnic."

"We'll have to hope the rain holds off." Reuben tied his horse to a nearby fence post, helped her down, took the blanket under his arm and took hold of the picnic basket. "You choose the place," he said to Cassandra.

"How about over there under that tree? And if it rains we'll have some shelter."

"Never go under a tree in a storm," he said.

She looked up at the sky, smiling. "There's no storm."

"It should be okay then." Reuben spread the blanket out and they both sat down. "If it rains, we'll have to brave the spiders," he said with a teasing grin.

“No spiders allowed! Can I open the basket?" Cassandra asked.

When he nodded, she opened it to see fruit and sandwiches, along with a bottle of red grape juice and two glasses.

"Where did you get the time to do all this?" she asked.

"I made time."

She giggled as she unscrewed the lid of the grape juice and poured them each a glass.

"Isn't the man supposed to do that?" he asked.

"I don't know, but I know I can't do everything. I poured the drinks so you can serve the food."

"Oh, it's like that is it? Will I have to do everything in this relationship?" He smiled and looked up at her.

She giggled. "I didn't know we were having a relationship."

"A friendship is a relationship. Unless you want it to be something more?"

She smiled back at him. And then she was lost for words. She wished she had some witty comeback to his lively banter, but what if she was taking it more seriously than he was?

"I'm sorry; this is probably too quick for you, considering the death of your boyfriend."

"*Nee,* it's not that. Things weren't good between us before he died— quite awhile before he died."

"I see." Reuben nodded, but the mood had changed. "I need to say something to you, Cassandra, and I know this is probably going to come as a surprise for you and you'll probably think I'm moving too fast, but I've never met a woman quite like you. I feel so easy and natural speaking with you. I feel like I've known you forever."

"I feel the same about you."

"Do you?"

She nodded. "I do." Cassandra looked into the sincerity of his eyes. She knew if she said the word that they would be boyfriend and girlfriend, but she couldn't have things progress that fast, not when he didn't know her secret. She had to stall things in some way, or should she tell him right now?

She decided. "There's something I need to tell you and I don't know how you're going to take it."

"Why so serious? It can't be that bad."

"It's quite bad. You see, when Jake and I were on *rumspringa* we lived together." There, she'd said it.

His jaw dropped. "That must've taken a lot of courage to tell me that. I respect honesty over everything else."

Seeing how badly he'd taken that part of the news, she couldn't bring herself to tell him what had resulted from her living with Jake. Maybe if she spent a few more weeks with Reuben, he would be so much in love with her that nothing would stand between them.

"So does that change how you feel about me?" she asked.

"Have you been baptized?"

She shook her head. "I was only back in the community for a couple of days before I decided to come and stay with Aunt Maud. I talked to the bishop about being baptized here." News of her talking to the bishop about being baptized put a smile on his face.

"You did?"

She smiled, and he leaned forward and picked up a glass and together they clinked glasses.

"Is Jake the closest you came to getting married?" he asked.

She nodded. "*Jah,* and you?"

"I've taken a few girls on buggy rides, but it never came

to anything. I've been told I'm too fussy. But then I met you, and you're everything that I asked for."

She stared at him, wondering if he was joking but there was no hint of a smile on his face. "I'm not perfect you know, Reuben. I've made many mistakes and done some dreadful things."

Then he laughed.

"I'm trying to be serious with you and you won't stop making me laugh."

He laughed some more and she could do nothing else but laugh with him.

When their laughter died down, he unwrapped sandwiches and placed two on each plate.

"These are chicken sandwiches."

"They look delicious," Cassandra said.

After they had eaten lunch, they walked down along the riverbank. She thought he was close to asking her to marry him, but he never did. Just a few more weeks and surely he'd be truly in love with her, and then she would tell him.

CHAPTER 19

Let no corrupt communication proceed out of your mouth,
but that which is good to the use of edifying,
that it may minister grace unto the hearers.
Ephesians 4:29

A MONTH FLEW BY, and Reuben and Cassandra had grown closer. He had no idea of the secret Cassandra was keeping from him.

"Where's Reuben?" Cassandra asked when she sat down to dinner and there was no sign of him. She noticed Maud and Max look at each other.

"He'll be a little late," Maud said.

"Is there something wrong?" Cassandra asked looking again between the two of them.

"*Nee,* there's nothing wrong," Max insisted.

Just as they started eating, the sound of a buggy coming to the house rang through the kitchen.

"You've got visitors," Cassandra said.

"Noo, you've got the visitor," Maud said with a smile.

Cassandra frowned at her. "What do you mean? Is it Jenny?" The only other visitor might be Bishop John or his wife, Ruth.

Max stood up. "Come, see for yourself."

Cassandra followed Maud and Max to the front door. It was Max's buggy driven by Reuben. Cassandra looked harder and saw someone sitting beside him.

When the buggy stopped, a young lady got out.

Cassandra's heart nearly stopped. It was Gretchen.

Maud explained, "Reuben was kind enough to collect her from the station. We wanted to surprise you for your birthday tomorrow, but it'll have to be an early surprise."

Cassandra forced a smile as Gretchen ran toward her.

"Cassandra!" Gretchen hugged Cassandra and because everyone was watching the two of them, Cassandra had to pretend to be pleased to see her.

"What a shock. You came all this way. How lovely!"

"Yes, it's your birthday tomorrow so *Mamm* thought you'd like to have one of us with you. *Mamm* doesn't like long journeys, so I said I'd go instead."

Gretchen greeted Maud and Max.

Maud put her arm around Gretchen, "Come on inside. I'll set another place at the table now that we don't have to keep your visit a secret."

Cassandra stopped and looked at Reuben, who was leading the horse to the barn. She walked over to him. *"Denke* for collecting her."

He could barely look at her. "That's fine. You're welcome."

"Why don't you leave the horse and come in for dinner. You can fix him up later," Cassandra said.

"Can't do that. The horse needs to be rubbed down."

By his abrupt tone, Cassandra knew something was wrong. Had Gretchen told him her secret? Is that why he was being so distant and cold?

He looked up at her. "Can you let Maud know I've eaten already? I won't join you all for dinner."

"Sure, I'll let her know." Cassandra walked away fighting back tears. If he couldn't accept the child she was carrying, then he was not the man for her. And if he were not the man for her, then there was no one. Adopting the baby out was now the only option. She'd been silly to build her hopes on Reuben before she'd told him the truth.

Cassandra sniffed, and wiped her eyes before she joined the other three in the kitchen. "Reuben said he's already eaten."

"Okay," Maud said.

Cassandra sat down and ate what she could. Even though she'd lost her appetite, she knew she had to eat for the sake of her unborn child.

As soon as she got her sister alone, she'd ask her what she'd told Reuben.

"Your *schweschder's* been quite busy here. We've been making pies and selling them at a roadside stall," Maud told Gretchen.

"Gut! Can I help? It sounds like fun."

Cassandra nodded because she could barely speak. Only Gretchen could think that working sounded like fun.

"An extra pair of hands is always a *gut* thing," Max said.

"Wait 'til I tell *Mamm* what you've been up to," Gretchen said.

"What do you mean?" Cassandra asked narrowing her eyes. Did she mean she'd tell her mother she was interested in a man? What exactly had Reuben told her sister?

"The pies, silly."

"Oh," Cassandra said as she looked back down at the food on her plate.

"Do you feel unwell, Cassandra?" Maud asked.

Cassandra nodded. "I do. All of a sudden, I feel sick."

"That's a shame," Max said.

"It happens like that. Why don't you go and lie down?" Maud suggested.

"I'll come and see you later to see if you want anything," Gretchen said.

"Denke, I think a lie down might do me good."

Cassandra walked to her room feeling sick to her stomach. What was her mother thinking sending Gretchen there? She'd have to know that would be the worst thing in the world. When had she and Gretchen ever gotten along?

An hour had passed before there was a small knock on her door.

"Jah?" Cassandra answered.

"It's me."

"What do you want?"

Gretchen walked in and sat on her bed. "How are you feeling?"

"Don't act like you care."

"I do, of course, I do."

Cassandra sat up in bed. "What did you say to Reuben?"

"It's not my fault. I thought he knew already."

She was right. Her secret was no longer a secret. "What exactly did you say?"

"I just said something about the *boppli* and I hoped you weren't big and fat when I saw you. I can't remember exactly."

Cassandra groaned.

"Do you like Reuben?"

"Jah, I do, but now that's not going to work—like everything else in my life—thanks to you." She stared at her sister. Gretchen was fair and pretty, and was always perfectly dressed with not a strand of hair finding it's way from beneath her *kapp.* "Why are you here anyway?"

"It's your birthday tomorrow."

"Since when has anyone cared about that?"

"Mamm was worried about you."

"It's a little late for that. They just sent me away without a care."

"That's not so and you know it."

"What I know is that my life is ruined and now with you opening your big mouth to Reuben it's doubly ruined."

"He would've found out."

"I know, but it was better to have it come from me. Can't you see that? I don't know what he thinks of me now. He could barely speak to me."

Gretchen shrugged. "Sorry. Can I do anything to fix it?"

"Jah, you can go home."

"I just got here. I don't want to make that long trip again for a few weeks."

"You're staying for weeks?"

Gretchen nodded. "I thought you'd be pleased."

Cassandra shook her head. "Why would I?"

Gretchen stood. "Why are you always so mean to me? I've come all this way so you wouldn't be by yourself on your birthday, and you're still mean and horrid to me."

"The sooner I get rid of you and rid of this," she placed her hands on her stomach, "the better off my life will be."

"You can't mean that."

"I do. How can I have a proper life and find a *gut mann* when he finds out what happened to me."

"If you love someone you can tell them all your secrets."

"Get out, Gretchen. Just go. My life's bad enough without you talking about things you know nothing about. You think you know everything and you know nothing."

Gretchen opened her mouth to speak.

Cassandra lay back on the bed. "Just go."

"Were you going to tell him?"

"Of course, I was. He's living in the *grossdaddi haus,* I can hardly keep it a secret."

"Well, tell him that."

"I can't. I had the perfect opportunity to tell him weeks ago and I didn't."

"*Gott* forgives and says we should forgive too."

Cassandra was growing more irritated with her sister every moment. "Yeah, well you should tell Reuben that not me." She picked up a pillow and threw it at her sister.

Gretchen picked up the pillow, which had fallen to the floor, and placed it on the bed before she walked out of the room closing the door behind her.

CASSANDRA DECIDED first thing in the morning she'd have Maud call Jenny and fast-track these meetings with potential parents for her baby.

CHAPTER 20

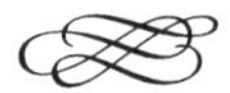

God is not a man, that he should lie;
neither the son of man, that he should repent:
hath he said, and shall he not do it?
or hath he spoken, and shall he not make it good?
Numbers 23:19

CASSANDRA HAD SLEPT IN. She knew it when she woke up and saw that the sky was dark gray. If it had been a bright sunny day, the light would have woken her.

She hurried out to breakfast, but there was only Gretchen at the table.

"Gretchen, where's Maud?"

"She said she had some errands to run. It's just me and you."

"Great!" Cassandra said sarcastically as she fell into a chair.

Gretchen rose to her feet. "I'll get you something to eat

and then I'll tell you what Reuben said about you this morning."

Cassandra jumped up and grabbed Gretchen's arm. "You spoke to him this morning?"

Gretchen pulled her arm out of Cassandra's grasp. "That hurt! *Jah,* I did!"

"What did he say?"

Gretchen put her hands on her hips. "I was trying to help you."

"Ach nee! What happened?" Cassandra sank into the chair knowing that she wasn't going to hear good news.

"I told him you were going to tell him."

"What did he say?"

"He said you should've told him already, but he understands why you didn't."

Cassandra smiled. "So, he's not mad at me?"

"Nee, he didn't seem to be."

"Denke, Gretchen. That's great news."

"Then he said something about he might be moving on soon. He's looking for someone else to finish the job he's doing for Maud and Max."

"What!" Cassandra shrieked. "That's not *gut!"*

"Well, don't yell at me. It's all your fault."

"I'll be in my room." Cassandra hurried to her room because she didn't want Gretchen to see her cry. Now all her hopes of marrying Reuben were dashed to pieces and it was all Gretchen's fault. It would've been a horrible shock for Reuben to find out that news from someone else.

"I've got some breakfast here for you, Cassandra."

"Leave it outside."

"Can I come in?"

"Nee, stay away from me," Cassandra said.

When she didn't hear anything for a while, she opened the door. There was no sign of Gretchen. Her eyes dropped to the tray of food that Gretchen had left for her. She leaned down to pick up the tray, and her belly was seized in a sharp, breath-stopping pain. Cassandra clutched at her stomach and screamed. "Gretchen!" She heard Gretchen's footsteps.

"What is it? What's wrong?"

"Pain," Cassandra managed to say.

"What will I do? No one's here."

Cassandra was certain she was losing the baby, but she couldn't. She closed her eyes and prayed for the life of her baby. For the first time in her life, she cared more for the life of her baby than her own. "Go to the barn and find the number of the midwife, Jenny."

"Should I call 911?"

"Jah, do it; go now."

BY THE TIME the paramedics arrived, Cassandra was sitting on the couch. She said she was a little better, but they insisted she go to the hospital for tests. They told her it could be an ectopic pregnancy, which would be dangerous for both herself and her baby. All the way in the ambulance she prayed that she wouldn't lose her baby.

She faded away, and passed out in the ambulance. When she came to, she was in a hospital bed.

"What happened?" she asked a nurse in uniform who was standing close by.

"You fainted."

"Is my baby okay?"

"You're both fine. We did an ultrasound and you're both doing well."

"It's not an ectopic pregnancy?"

The nurse shook her head. "No. The doctor wants to keep you in overnight, though, and you should be alright to go home in the morning."

Cassandra silently thanked God. "What caused the pain?"

"The doctor thinks it was round ligament pain, which often occurs in the second trimester as the baby grows. It can be pretty intense."

"So that's normal?"

"Yes. There's no need to worry. I'll be back to take your blood pressure in an hour. Your blood pressure was a little low and the paramedics said you hadn't had anything to eat this morning."

"That's right."

"That's why we've got you on an intravenous drip. It'll make you feel better and replace any fluids you've lost."

She looked down at her hand where the drip was attached.

"Press this button if you'd like someone to help you to the bathroom."

"Okay."

Then the nurse left her alone. Cassandra looked around the room. There were four beds, but one was empty. The other two had old ladies in them and they were asleep.

It was after lunch was served that Maud and Gretchen

came to see her. Cassandra had never been so pleased to see her sister.

"I'm okay and so is the *boppli.* Thank you for helping us, Gretchen."

"You gave us a fright," Maud said as Gretchen hugged Cassandra.

"I gave myself a fright."

Someone else walked into the room and Cassandra looked over to see who it was. It was Reuben.

"Maud, why don't we find that coffee shop that we were told was in the hospital?"

"Jah, we shall," Maud agreed with Gretchen.

When the two ladies were out of the room, Reuben came forward taking off his hat. "I'm so sorry, I've been such an idiot."

"Nee, you haven't been."

He shook his head. "It was such a shock to hear from Gretchen something I thought you should've told me. You could've told me, you know."

"I was going to tell you, but I was ashamed of getting into this situation without being married."

"You weren't alone in that. You had help from a certain man. A certain man who, you told me, left you when he returned to your community without you. Did he know about the *boppli?"*

"He did."

"I hope you will still... This is harder than I thought. Can we take up where we left off?"

"I don't know. I've got a big decision to make and I must do what I think is best for the *boppli.* I might be finding a couple to adopt the baby." As much as she felt she was in love with Reuben, she couldn't allow him to distract her from the big decision she had to make. Jake had left her, and Reuben had nearly left her. She couldn't allow herself or her baby to be subject to the whim of a man.

He shook his head. "Don't do that, Cassandra. Don't give up your *boppli.* You might regret it forever."

"I might, but I'll do it if that's what's best."

"Best for whom?"

"The baby is all that matters to me now."

He stepped forward and crouched down by her bed. "I've hurt you."

She looked into his eyes. Yes, he'd hurt her. Who did she have she could rely on? It seemed there was no one.

"I want us to be like we were before."

"Before you knew about the baby?"

He nodded.

"We can't. You told my *schweschder* you were going to leave."

"I'm sorry, from the bottom of my heart, I'm sorry. You must find it in your heart to forgive me, Cassandra."

She nodded. She'd like to forgive him. "I'll try."

"When I heard you were in the hospital it was like a knife was searing through my heart. I realized then I don't want to be without you—ever. Would you marry me, Cassandra?"

Her jaw dropped open. He wanted to marry her?

"I will never leave you. I'll always stay by your side and look after you and your baby. We can raise the *boppli* together. I think I'd be a *gut dat.*"

This was what she'd always wanted, but now she was

too tired to think properly. "I think that's what I want, but I'm so tired."

He stood up, leaned over and kissed her on her forehead. "I'll give you all the time you need." He shook his head. "I can't help thinking this was all my fault."

Was that why he was asking her to marry him—out of guilt? She would've asked him, but she was growing too tired to speak.

"I'm going to collect you tomorrow morning. We spoke to the doctor in the hallway and he said you'd be going home. Do you mind if I'm the one who comes for you?"

"That's fine," Cassandra managed to say before her eyes closed.

CHAPTER 21

But my God shall supply all your need
according to his riches in glory by Christ Jesus.
Philippians 4:19

CASSANDRA WOKE in the hospital a few hours later. She had a dim memory of Reuben asking her to marry him.

She lay there feeling sorry for herself. As much as she wanted to keep the baby, she knew she had to do what was best. Maybe 'best' was giving the baby away to someone—someone with a stable home. Her baby deserved to grow up in a loving home, as she'd had.

She'd been horrible to her parents and her younger sister for years, and for what? Tears poured down her cheeks as she thought of all the horrible things she'd done throughout her life. She hadn't made things easier for Jake; she had talked him into going on *rumspringa* when he hadn't wanted to. Now he was gone, she couldn't even say she was sorry. She wasn't about to ruin another man's life.

Ideally, she'd want to keep the baby, but she had no job, no home, and no money to raise a baby with. Reuben had come into her life when she hadn't expected him. Maybe God had blessed her with a gift. With Reuben, she might find a second chance for happiness. Cassandra closed her eyes tightly and prayed that things would work out the very best for her baby, herself, and for Reuben.

What if God had designed this before the beginning of time, that she and Reuben should or would raise this child together? Just because she had made mistakes didn't mean she couldn't turn her life around—right a wrong and live a good life. She opened her heart to God and confessed how selfish and mean she'd been to people. Now that she was carrying a child, she knew how it felt to carry the responsibility of another life. Slowly, bit-by-bit deep in her heart, Cassandra knew she wouldn't want to be treated by this child how she'd treated her parents.

She'd been horrid to her sister who'd come all that way to see her.

Cassandra knew the only way out of this was to turn her life over to God and let Him work it out—and right there in her hospital bed, of all places to be spending her twentieth birthday, that is what she did.

When she opened her eyes, she knew she had to trust God to see her through and show her the right way to go.

IT WAS the next morning that Reuben came to collect her.

As soon as Reuben had entered the room, her heart brightened. This was the man for her and she knew it.

"How are you?"

She was sitting fully dressed on the bed. "The doctor came and saw me early this morning and said I'm good to go home."

He sat next to her. "Do you need to rest?"

"He didn't mention it, but I won't be running any marathons."

He nodded. "Good to know. I'll cancel the one I entered you in next week."

She giggled. *"Jah,* please do."

Reuben looked down and took her hand. Then, he looked into her eyes. "I always want to be by your side, looking after you, Cassandra."

"You do?"

He nodded. "I know I said I wouldn't pressure you…"

"But now you're going to?"

When he glanced over at the people in the other beds, Cassandra leaned in and whispered, "Don't mind them. They're not listening."

"I want to marry you; and then, if you want we'll go back to your community and live there, or we'll stay here."

"You've thought it through?"

"I've been thinking of little else since I first saw you in Max and Maud's kitchen."

She raised her eyebrows. "Really?"

He nodded. "Why don't we get married now, before the *boppli's* born?"

"You'd marry me and raise the *boppli* with me?"

"I can't think of anything I'd rather do."

She smiled and looked down at their clasped hands. When she looked up at him, she asked, "And this is not offered out of guilt or pity?"

"Not at all. It's out of love. I've never felt this way before. I'd never known love before I met you. Will you marry me, Cassandra Yoder?"

She inhaled deeply. She'd prayed all night for the best outcome and she could not have imagined a better outcome than this. The man she loved would become her husband and he was happy about raising her child as their child. "I will. I will marry you. This must be the best birthday gift ever."

He put an arm around her and pulled her tightly toward him, kissing her gently on her forehead. "Happy birthday, a day late. Shall we go to see the bishop soon? I'd say today, but I think you should take it easy. I'll go and speak to the bishop for both of us."

"Would you?" Cassandra wanted to marry him as soon as she could.

"Let's get out of here, and I'll go and talk with the bishop as soon as you're safely back at Maud's."

WHEN THEY GOT BACK to Maud's, Reuben told Maud and Gretchen the good news even before he left to speak to the bishop.

"That's *wunderbaar* news," Maud said.

"I'm so happy for both of you," Gretchen said. "And where will you live?"

"We haven't decided yet," Cassandra said. "We're

having the *boppli* here in Oakes County. If that's still going to be okay with you, Aunt Maud."

"It's perfect."

"*Gut.* I feel comfortable with Jenny and I don't want to change things now."

Reuben said, "I probably should have spoken to the bishop first, but we were excited." He looked lovingly at Cassandra.

"Well, go ask—or tell him now," Cassandra ordered.

He laughed and said to Maud, "She's giving me orders already."

"That's something you'll have to get used to," Gretchen said, laughing too.

They all laughed, and then Reuben headed off to speak with the bishop.

Maud put her arm around Cassandra. "Come and lie down on the couch. I'll get you a blanket. Unless you'd rather lie down in your bedroom."

"The couch sounds good, *denke.*"

Once Cassandra was comfortable on the couch, Maud and Gretchen wanted to hear all about her romance with Reuben.

"Of course, I could tell it was going to happen. I knew there was something there the moment you laid eyes on each other."

Cassandra laughed. "The good thing is that now I can keep the *boppli.*"

"When will you tell *Mamm* and Dat?" Gretchen asked.

"I don't know. I want to get married without a lot of people around. I might not tell *Mamm* and *Dat* until after the wedding."

“You can’t do that, Cassandra,” Gretchen said.

“I can if that’s what I want. Reuben doesn’t have any *familye,* so I don’t want a whole lot of my *familye* there to remind him that he doesn’t have any.”

“Okay.” Gretchen nodded. “That’s very thoughtful of you.”

“Reuben is going to ask the bishop if we can get married soon. The bishop already knows I’m pregnant.”

“That’s *gut.”* Maud nodded.

“The best thing is that I can keep my *boppli.* Things couldn’t have turned out any better.”

“Weeping may endure for a night, but joy comes in the morning,” Maud said.

“Jah, everything looked bad for me and now I’m so happy. Except I’m still scared about the birth.”

“But you’ll have the baby in your arms as soon as it’s all over. And you’ll never have to give it away to anyone.”

“Not ‘it,’ Gretchen, him or her.” Cassandra smiled thinking how she once called the baby "it" and her mother had sorely objected. Now Cassandra was attached to her unborn child in a way she never knew she would be.

It was two hours later when Reuben arrived back at the house. Maud and Gretchen had made themselves scarce so Reuben and Cassandra could speak alone.

“What did he say?” was the first thing Cassandra asked when Reuben walked in the door.

“How are you feeling?”

“Fine. What did he say?”

He sat on the floor beside the couch and held her hand. "We will be married one week from today."

"He said we could?"

"Jah, he did. And he wants to hold your baptism before that."

"Did he give you a hard time or ask you a lot of questions?"

"He did, and of course he wants to speak to you too. I said I'd drive you there in a couple days when you feel better."

Relief washed over Cassandra. Everything was turning out well. She was even pleased that Gretchen was there in the house.

CHAPTER 22

But the fruit of the Spirit is love, joy, peace, patience, kindness, goodness,
faithfulness, gentleness, self-control; against such things there is no law.
Galatians 5:22-23

CASSANDRA AND REUBEN had been married for a couple of months and living in Maud and Max's *grossdaddi haus* when the time came. Cassandra felt her first contraction.

"I don't know if I can do this," she said once she'd woken Reuben up.

"You can. You're a strong woman and you can do anything. Do you want me to go and fetch Maud and Gretchen?"

"*Jah* please."

Reuben hurried out of the house. It was only an hour after everyone had gone to bed. Gretchen had stayed on and had taken over the pie making for their roadside stall that Cassandra had begun and hadn't been able to follow through with. Cassandra was having the baby at a birthing center with the midwife, Jenny, attending her, and Reuben was to be present as well. Maud had decided Cassandra should share this event only with her husband, who had chosen to accept this child as his own.

Five hours later, Cassandra was at the birth center and Reuben was holding her hand. She felt as if she couldn't go on. The pains were coming hard and fast. When she was sure she'd have to ask for a C-section, the pains stopped.

"What's happening now? I just want the baby out!"

Jenny explained, "You're transitioning. The first stage is over and your *boppli* will be here soon."

"Will I have to push?"

After Jenny had examined her, she said, "You're fully dilated, so you can push whenever you feel the urge."

"But I don't."

Reuben stroked her arm. "Keep calm. She didn't say you had to do it right away. Just do it when you feel ready to."

Cassandra nodded and calmed herself by looking into Reuben's eyes. "Okay, okay."

Fifteen minutes later, Cassandra felt the first urges to push.

The baby slithered into the world half an hour later. Jenny put the baby directly onto Cassandra's chest.

She hugged her baby as love surged through her body.

It was a feeling she'd never had before. This was her child, and she would do anything to look after and protect this small infant in her arms—anything. To Cassandra's delight, her baby's head was covered in dark hair. Now there would be someone else with dark hair in the family besides her and Maud. "Is it a boy?"

"See for yourself," the midwife said.

It didn't matter. Boy or girl, love had filled Cassandra's heart.

Reuben kissed Cassandra's forehead. Her world was complete. God had turned her life around in a few short months. *"Denke,"* she said aloud to God.

"Do you want to cut the cord, Reuben?" the midwife said.

"Me?" He looked at Cassandra, who nodded.

Reuben took the scissors and cut the cord where Jenny directed him. "Did you see what our baby is?" he asked Cassandra while the midwife was clamping the baby's cord.

"A girl?"

"Jah, a girl."

They'd already picked out names. It was Jasmine now that they knew she was a girl, and if they'd had a boy, they'd planned to call him Michael.

"She's so beautiful, just like her *Mamm."* Reuben kissed Cassandra again. "I should make some phone calls and tell everyone."

Cassandra couldn't stop looking at her baby. It was an odd feeling to have a baby that was hers—she was a miracle—every baby was a miracle. She'd done the right thing and written to Jake's parents about the baby, but they hadn't written back. Perhaps they hadn't gotten the letter, or perhaps they didn't want to know the truth. She'd visit them when she returned to her old community and make certain that the letter hadn't gone astray. And then, if they didn't want to know, she wouldn't push it on them. As far as everyone else was concerned, the baby was hers and Reuben's.

Reuben took Cassandra and the baby home later that day—back to the *grossdaddi haus* where they had been living.

Maud and Gretchen rushed in as soon as they got home.

"Where is he?" Maud said, rushing in first and followed close behind by Gretchen.

"It's a girl!" Cassandra said holding the baby close.

Aunt Maud said, "I know, I know. I've been so used to saying 'he.' Can I hold her?"

Cassandra passed the small bundle to Aunt Maud. "She's so sweet. Look at her, Gretchen."

Gretchen stared at the baby. "There's never been a sweeter *boppli.*" Gretchen turned to look at Cassandra, and then sat down beside her. "Was the birth awful?"

"Like they say, you quickly forget it when you're holding your *boppli.* Let's just say I wouldn't want to go through it again too soon." Cassandra gave a little laugh.

Reuben walked into the room.

"A letter came for you, Reuben. It's from Cassandra's parents."

Reuben and Cassandra exchanged glances. They'd talked about how upset her parents might have been, not being invited to the wedding and being informed of it only after the event.

"Where's the letter?" he asked.

"Can you fetch it for him, Gretchen?"

Gretchen left to get the letter from the main house. When Gretchen returned, she handed the unopened letter to Reuben.

He opened it and read it. Cassandra watched as tears formed in his eyes.

That was it! If they wouldn't accept him, then she could not return home. Reuben was her family now, along with their baby.

"What does it say?" Cassandra asked.

"They said they're delighted about the marriage. They'd like us to come home—well, you to come home with me—and your vadder would like me to work with him on the farm. They said we could live with them until we find a place of our own. Or we can live in their *gross-daddi haus* if we want." Reuben sniffed.

Cassandra knew it was because he'd never had family, and the idea of working side by side with her father meant a lot to him. Reuben turned away and Cassandra blinked back tears of her own.

"Would you like to hold her now, Gretchen?"

"I certainly would." Gretchen stood and Maud handed the baby over to her.

"Are you going back home, Cassandra?" Gretchen asked.

"I think so. What about you, Gretchen? Will you be able to leave the pies?"

Gretchen glanced over at Maud and smiled. "I think

I'd like to stay a little longer. Is that all right with you, Aunt Maud?"

"I'd like nothing better. And we've grown quite a thriving demand for our pies."

Cassandra giggled. It had been her idea to make the pies and now Gretchen and her aunt were consumed daily in making their pies—and loving it.

CHAPTER 23

The Lord is slow to anger and abounding in steadfast love,
forgiving iniquity and transgression,
but he will by no means clear the guilty,
visiting the iniquity of the fathers on the children,
to the third and the fourth generation
Numbers 14:18

WHEN THEIR BABY was old enough to travel, Cassandra and Reuben made their way back to Lancaster County. So much had happened in the few short months after her return from *rumspringa.* She'd gotten baptized, gotten married, and had a baby. And she'd learned how to get along with Gretchen. Gretchen had stayed on with Aunt Maud and Uncle Max.

The last leg of their journey was by taxi. Cassandra couldn't stop smiling when her old white house with the red roof came into view.

She was a different person from the girl who'd gone there months ago to deliver some dreadful news to her parents. God had healed her heart and given her the gifts of a child and a husband.

When the car stopped, Reuben paid the driver, who then lifted their luggage out of the trunk while Reuben helped Cassandra and their baby from the car.

Cassandra's parents came outside the house to greet them.

"*Mamm,* this is Reuben."

Her parents smiled and shook Reuben's hand, introducing themselves before they turned their attention to Jasmine.

Cassandra's mother lifted the baby out of her hands and hugged her to herself. "She's just like you as a *boppli,* Cassandra. Your hair was as dark as this."

"I know, and Aunt Maud has dark hair—or did have once. I took after Aunt Maud. I'll miss her."

"Looks like we're going to have some more dark-haired *grosskin,* then," her mother said.

"Give them a chance to settle in first." Mr. Yoder laughed at his wife and then put his hand on Reuben's shoulder. "Let's get this luggage inside. And then, we've got a lot to talk about."

While Reuben and Cassandra's father took the luggage up the stairs, the women went into the kitchen. Cassandra sat at the table.

"You've done well," her mother said to her.

"*Denke, Mamm. Gott* turned my life around."

Cassandra's mother chuckled. "It took you a while to

get there, but now you've arrived. You know that nothing will turn out right until you put Him first."

As much as Cassandra wasn't used to agreeing with her mother, she knew that she was right.

"I'm so glad everything turned out well and I met Reuben. I didn't have to give my *boppli* away. I can raise her myself. It's a blessing."

"You'll be a blessing to Jasmine."

"Do you mean that, *Mamm?*"

"Of course, I do. Your *vadder* has been so excited to have a son-in-law who's agreed to work the farm with him. Do you know what that's like for him to have a man living here under this roof after so many girls?"

Cassandra shook her head. *"Nee,* I don't. I suppose it'll make things easier for *Dat* and he'll have someone to talk to besides you."

"He's so happy since he got that letter back from Reuben saying he'd work here."

"We might not live here for too long. We'll get our own place, but we won't go far away."

"You can always stay in the *grossdaddi haus* if you need some more space before you move."

Cassandra smiled. She wanted to be close to her parents in the house, but she didn't want to let them know that. She'd always been so prickly toward them that she didn't want to shock them too much by how she'd changed.

"When will she wake?" her mother asked, staring down at Jasmine.

"Soon. She's due for a feeding, so she'll wake soon."

Her mother sat down at the kitchen table next to her.

"Mamm, I will go and visit Jake's parents soon. I sent them a letter, but they didn't answer."

"You told them about the *boppli?"*

"It was best. I felt that was the right thing to do. I thought maybe they didn't get the letter."

"Maybe."

"Will you take me there tomorrow? I know Reuben's keen to start work with *Dat."*

"I will. It just makes things awkward. If they didn't know, then everyone could think she's Reuben's."

"She is, she's his too."

"You know what I mean."

"I'm sorry, *Mamm.* I didn't want to hurt you or *Dat.* I never thought things through."

"I know. When you're young, it's not so easy to think of consequences. These things take time and sometimes we have to learn from our mistakes."

Cassandra nodded.

Reuben came into the kitchen with Mr. Yoder.

When Mr. Yoder looked over his wife's shoulder at the baby, Reuben whispered to Cassandra, "We're all going to get along fine."

Cassandra looked up at Reuben's smiling face, thankful that her parents had welcomed him with open arms.

THE NEXT DAY, Mrs. Yoder drove Cassandra to Jake's parents' house, and stayed in the buggy with Jasmine while Cassandra knocked on their door.

Jake's mother opened the door and didn't look pleased to see her. "Hello, Cassandra."

"Hello, can I come in?"

She wedged herself in the doorway. "Are you back for good?"

"I'm here with my husband and we plan to stay. Did you get my letter about the *boppli?*"

"What do you want, Cassandra? Isn't it enough that you made Jake go with you on *rumspringa?* He told us he didn't want to go, but he went because he thought he'd lose you."

"Jah, and then he came back. The baby is your *grosskin."*

"My husband and I would prefer if you kept that to yourself."

Cassandra frowned. "You can't mean that."

"Don't put shame on my son's name by naming him as the *vadder."*

"It's not about shame, it's about your *grosskin."*

She shook her head. "Leave my son out of this please, Cassandra. Just go and live your life with your husband and child. And please, leave Jake out of it."

"You don't want anyone to know?"

She shook her head again and closed the door without saying goodbye. It was a strange response, but maybe they were still grieving over Jake. She got back into the buggy and told her mother what had happened.

Her mother picked up the reins and clicked the horse onward. "It's less complicated this way. No one wants to talk about things that bring shame."

Cassandra sighed. She'd just been trying to do the

right thing. She looked down at Jasmine. "This little girl has plenty of people who love her."

"She certainly does."

On the way back to the house, Cassandra saw her husband in the fields working alongside her father. "Look, *Mamm.*" She pointed at the two of them.

Her mother stopped the buggy and together they watched the two men.

"Your *vadder* finally has a son. That's what he always wanted."

Cassandra laughed. "Aw, *Mamm, Dat's* got many sons-in-law."

"They all have their own farms to work, or their own jobs. Reuben was the only one who took up your *vadder's* offer to work the farm. I've never seen him happier."

"They do look happy together. Reuben's always wanted a *familye* and now he has a large one. He'll be overwhelmed when he meets all of them." As Cassandra stared at her father and Reuben, she finally felt at peace with her parents and her family. She'd found where she was meant to be and whom she was meant to be with. Reuben had changed not only her life but her parents' lives. In turn, Reuben had been blessed with a wife, a baby and a large extended family. At that moment, Cassandra thanked God that he'd turned her life around and had made everything right.

Therefore I say unto you,
What things soever ye desire,
when ye pray, believe that ye receive them,

and ye shall have them.
Mark 11:24

Thank you for reading
Amish Widow's Secret
Expectant Amish Widows Book 9.

~

EXPECTANT AMISH WIDOWS

Book 1 Amish Widow's Hope

Book 2 The Pregnant Amish Widow

Book 3 Amish Widow's Faith

Book 4 Their Son's Amish Baby

Book 5 Amish Widow's Proposal

Book 6 The Pregnant Amish Nanny

Book 7 A Pregnant Widow's Amish Vacation

Book 8 The Amish Firefighter's Widow

Book 9 Amish Widow's Secret

Book 10 The Middle-Aged Amish Widow

Book 11 Amish Widow's Escape

Book 12 Amish Widow's Christmas

Book 13 Amish Widow's New Hope

Book 14 Amish Widow's Story

Book 15 Amish Widow's Decision

Book 16 Amish Widow's Trust

Book 17 The Amish Potato Farmer's Widow

ABOUT SAMANTHA PRICE

A prolific author of Amish fiction, Samantha Price wrote stories from a young age, but it wasn't until later in life that she took up writing full time.

Samantha is happiest on her computer lost in the world of her characters. She best known for the Ettie Smith Amish Mysteries series and the Expectant Amish Widows series.

To learn more about Samantha Price and her books visit:

www.samanthapriceauthor.com

Samantha Price loves to hear from her readers. Connect with her at:

samanthaprice333@gmail.com

www.facebook.com/SamanthaPriceAuthor

Follow Samantha Price on BookBub

Twitter @ AmishRomance

www.pinterest.com/AmishRomance

Made in the USA
San Bernardino, CA
11 March 2019